The Shamanic Warrior

DAVID J. GREEN

Printed by:
Amazon Publishing Hub

ISBN: 978-1-916707-18-4

Table of Contents

I'd like to dedicate this book to my wife, whose unending support has helped me to fulfill another desire on my bucket list.

Acknowledgments

I would like to acknowledge all those ancient, slavish historians, who were probably coerced into recording accurate, or otherwise, the details of their forebears as much as was humanly possible. May all their efforts be appreciated, and for those interested enough to give thanks.

About the Author

David still works at 72 years of age, three days a week, teaching art subjects and also has a business in stained-glass art which he has been doing for 33 years. Writing has always been his love and this book began about 30 years ago, having been edited many times over. It began through an interest and curiosity about the dark ages and he chose another take on the life and times in which people lived and behaved, trying not to equate necessarily with present day too much. There are many elements which could be laboured over but he wanted to keep a certain pace in the events, leaving the reader's imagination to fill in the gaps.

DAVID J. GREEN

The Shamanic Warrior

CHAPTER ONE

Sanctuary

702 AD

A cold, pale light, the shape of an anchor, flashed upon the smooth face of a young Saxon girl as she spied out of the long-house shutter onto the snow-filled land. Her curiosity was piqued by the family's exceptionally large bear-like dog, lumbering at a little distance from his dishevelled master and a roaring fire. The dog raised his eyebrow and emitted a low growl. "What is it, Loki?" asked the girl as she stroked her soft hand over his half-pricked ear. Slowly he stretched, bending his back, and arching his buttocks, constantly staring towards the door.

It was late afternoon on a cold November day, grey and wild outside with snow blowing this way and that, the watery sun breaking through at odd intervals like a brilliant torch constantly being snuffed out. The bright white of the snow was hard on the eye compared to the gently lit glow of the large room, a light that was akin to the golden glow of the girl's hair. A strong scent of ale and freshly made bread filled the air, combined with the after-smell of farmyard stock, geese, cattle, pigs, and horses. Apart from the master and the girl of the house, everyone was busy, some servant women weaving and sewing in the large hall while others baking in the big kitchen of a rather unconventional Saxon Noble's home. To the rear, stable hands mucked out, tended horses, and cleaned armoury and horse finery.

Loki was growling more persistently now. Heavy black clouds followed as if to introduce the early evening darkness. Just as the girl was about to pull away from the shutter, she caught sight of a tall, hairy, bulking shape tramping down into the village, roughly a hundred paces away and covered half in snow, bedraggled but upright and aiming for the house. Fear rippled its cold talons through her spine as she suddenly screamed, "Father, c-c-come quick. An ogre is coming to kill us and steal our food!" The father, who was lightly dozing by the cosy glow of the fire, woke in an angry haze.

"What damn nonsense be it this time, girl?"

Many of the staff looked around, curious but not alarmed.

Loki started barking, his deep throaty bark, coughing at the same time, having been startled so suddenly by Inga's outburst. The rest of the dogs in the village were also alerted. The girl's mother and a couple of servants followed as her father stumbled towards the window, glancing quickly through the opening and plucking a large shiny axe from the wall. He headed to the door, unsure of what he might meet. Inga clung to her father's left sleeve as he bravely swung open the heavy wooden door. Loki tried to intervene, but Inga grabbed him in time, sliding across the floor slightly. Father stepped upon the veranda to challenge the stranger struggling in the blizzard, only to see a figure face down in the snow with a huge horse standing back at a small distance, its reins dragging along, looking confused and travel-weary as it shook its head, releasing a plume of snow with blood and sweat dripping from its nose.

The father signalled to the servants to bring the stranger into the house and take the horse to the stables. Mother, gathering her shawl, went outside to help with her maidservant, as she would, while the father snarled at her impetuousness. Inga joined her in attendance.

If he had not wrapped himself so well, the unconscious man beneath the bearskins and sodden wool would probably not have lived to tell his tale. He was blue and very stiff from a long, cold, excruciating journey. Mother examined him for frostbite, but he was lucky. Inga could not stop staring at his face all the time she was helping her mother to undress the stranger and place him near the fire on a soft, horse-hair mattress. As he was being tended to, the mother remarked how tall he was. "Everybody's tall to you, Bronwen," scoffed the father.

4

"Well, he's taller than you, Father!" Inga said cheekily. If his old war wound had not been gnawing at him, her father might not have been so amicable.

"Well, let's see if he can take any food and ale, wife." asked the master. He then shouted to his senior servant, "Aedric, what of the man's horse?"

Slowly entering the room, a man with a discernibly haughty attitude, Aedric answered, "He was hard to settle, sire. As I showed him a quiet corner, he became wild as if possessed, but when I tied him near the cows, he calmed down. His face has been freshly cut as well, sire, teeth marks ... not from any animal sire," adding sarcastically, "Do you think this rider was preparing to eat him?"

"WHAT, eat a horse while it's still staring you in the face, without cutting its throat first... you blethering fool?" retorted the master.

Inga giggled.

Aedric continued, he loved to annoy his master up to a certain point, "Well, the man may have been possessed by your dog's namesake, sire. There may be some mischievous spirit entering the man?"

The father, a no-nonsense man, unable to detect Aedric's deviousness, blasted, "And you may be dispossessed of your senses, you woolly-minded idiot! His horse waits around to be devoured. You should know as well as I, this horse is as loyal to his master as the master to him, a man of good regard, I would say. No, something is well amiss here!"

In a trice, the stranger was stripped bare, with Bronwen, Inga, and two of the servant women whisking away his garments, armour, and weapons placed near the hearth. Bronwen ordered one of her servants to have them cleaned and polished. Having had his cap removed, the platted hairstyle of a Jute warrior was revealed, but there was more; Inga was about to blurt out their sudden discovery when her mother tugged sharply on her pigtail and pressed her finger to Inga's lips. Two of the servant women held a silent look of surprise; they were then told to leave and say nothing. Aedric looked in their direction suspiciously but could not gain full sight due to large shelves of trinkets and furniture interrupting his vision.

Father knew something was odd straight away and dismissed Aedric swiftly, watching him to make sure the serf went away without excuse. "Make certain the steed has no more that ails him!" shouted the master.

He would have sold Aedric years ago if he wasn't so good at his job. His master was uncertain of how much he trusted the man, but Aedric always knew how far he could go and what to do to appease his master.

Bronwen wiped her brow and beckoned her husband over to see what the mystery was as she bathed the man. "Well, by the vexing spit of Woden, we do not need any more of them in the village," as his estimation of the stranger began to subside.

"I do not think he's quite what you think, my love. These marks are not all that they should be for a shaman; look there," as she pointed to his chest, "and there are bite marks on him too," cautioned Bronwen.

"What do you mean about the other marks, mother?" enquired Inga.

Just as Bronwen was about to speak, Loki stood up and came over to the stranger with a strange inquisitiveness he had not shown before. He then sniffed profusely, as if picking up some odd scent, when suddenly, the stranger's eyes gently opened. Inga quickly threw a blanket over him for fear of being caught staring at his nakedness while clumsily covering his face.

He pulled the blanket from his head and spoke softly, with a slightly stronger accent than his hosts, a smattering of the old Fatherland. "Where am I?" As a tall, square-shouldered figure with thick blonde hair stood over him.

Loki twisted his head in curiosity and then keenly sniffed the air again.

The father responded, "You are a guest in my house. I am Wenslau, Reeve of these lands, some 30,000 hectares ... with more to follow if my neighbours give me any more trouble and ..." Suddenly, a long heavy pounding came at the large door of a particular sound that gave him away.

"Let him in, wife!" said Wenslau immediately, aware of the visitor.

The door was half blown open with the freezing wind as Bronwen undid the latch. Standing in his vest and trousers was a ruddy-faced, ginger-haired man, squat, a mass of flesh and muscle with no discernible neck, which was probably why he mumbled so much, apart from the fact he always suffered with his teeth. "S-s-sire, I - I - saw someone approach as I was putting out the ashes."

He was Eich, the village blacksmith, a little out of breath with the climb up the village and the wind against him. "S-s-sire, is all w-well?" he asked in his wheezy manner. No sooner had the squat fellow got the words out of his mouth; there was another knock at the door, this time more lightly and with impatience.

"Tell that little fart to go away!" said Wenslau, knowing fully who his second visitor was. Eich laughed, his squeaky, hoarse laugh, all the time wreaking of sulphurous sweat. Inga avoided him at all costs.

Inga went to the spyhole on the door to tell the other visitor to go away. There, dancing on the porch as if needing to toilet, thwacking his arms and hands on his sides, was another even smaller figure with a mass of black hair, carpeted in snow and looking exactly like a little fat Inuit. He went by the name of Luuah, but nobody knew how to properly pronounce it. A very excitable little Pictish man, he spoke at a hundred miles an hour... badly! He saw the light of the spyhole open and said quickly, in his broken accent, "Plea no teww me go awaay, I have to teww mashter ... shome shpichious pe-apple come to top of viwwage looking shpichious, Meeng, shee too, shee witnessh, ma doggy!"

"Oh-oh-oh, let him in," said Wenslau reluctantly. Eich frowned instantly, as he didn't have much patience for

Luuah, partly because he couldn't either hear or understand him.

"Just wait till I question Meeng to see what she has to say," jibed Wenslau.

"Bu' she no tawk, shire!" everyone in the room chuckled; even the stranger raised a half-conscious smile.

"The problem and its resolution are before us," said Wenslau, "but be vigilant as you return to your homes, KEEP LOOKOUT that means Luuah too!" he added wryly.
Loki barked several times, deeply, once more, as if to add to his master's voice. "Tell all to go back to their homes!"

Darkness blanketed the village as lights seeped from veiled windows and through door cracks, revealing the many houses thereabouts, their smoky-wrapped rooftops swept by the wind and snow.

 At the top of the village, just slightly over its brow, were five scruffily hooded figures, three adults and two juveniles, their features almost hidden but for an occasional shimmer of light from the village beacon lights. The skin of the tallest member was a putrid yellow-white hue. They were very stealthy and able to creep quietly enough not to disturb any mortal thing. The two younger members attempted to sneak their way, awkwardly, down the back of the village amongst the gorse and bracken, but the tall one called them back in a low, blood-curdling growl.

That was their cue to leave quickly, as all the dogs of the village erupted once more. Luuah's four wives came out in turn, with Meeng, a skinny little curly-haired mutt, barking and wailing, trying to negotiate the deep snow with little success.

The women were all armed and used to fighting, especially the smallest one, Fryda. She ran out waving her short sword and axe like an Amazon, shouting for the intruders to dare show their faces. Hilda, the tallest of Luuah's wives and the quietest, tramped quickly over the brow of the hill, undaunted by what she might meet with just a spear for protection. Her eyesight was like a hawk's; in that darkness, she could make out maybe four or five figures and three ponies racing as fast as they could to distance themselves from the village. Grunhild, the eldest of Luuah`s wives, came up alongside and asked what Hilda had seen as Fryda was shouting with great bravado from ten paces behind how she would single-handedly rip out their entrails to feed to the swine!

Nearer to the house was Mildred, a young, strong-looking woman with striking blonde and red hair who remarked how she knew why Luuah chose Fryda ... they were so alike! Luuah could not join them as he was badly detained on the netty after eating something that did not agree with him.

After the fracas near Luuah's house, an entourage of armed villagers, headed by Wenslau, came to meet with Hilda to ask what she saw. Wenslau had brought Loki with him and made sure he had the scent of the intruders.

"We will seek them out at first light; the weather is already against us," said Wenslau, "return to your homes."

Just then, a tall, dark, hooded figure came up alongside the master. Wenslau knew these furtive steps, even on snow. "Is there ought I may do, sire?" enquired the man.

"Nay, Rowe, we may be lured to a trap; I want us properly prepared at first light. I fear this may have something to do with the stranger unless it's the workings of that devious monk again?" muttered Wenslau. Rowe was one of Wenslau's most trusted men and chief of his Huscarls, a friend and ally since childhood.

Everyone slowly returned to their respective homes except for one couple who were somewhat involved behind Eich's chimney, out of sight, forbidden from one another but finding any excuse to be together despite the inclement weather. The snow was all but stopped, though a harsh, cold wind swept through the village, and only Eich's workshop chimney would be warm enough, sheltered enough, and quiet enough to enjoy their brief courting.

Wenslau entered his home to find the stranger in new clothes with a wrap of fur around his shoulders and seated by the fire, shakily drinking a tonic prepared by Bronwen. He turned and smiled coyly at Wenslau, attempting to stand but being told to stay where he was.

"Sire, your kind wife has told me that you may have had some trouble about the village. I ..." Just as he was about to continue, a violent tremor overtook him.

"Be still," said Bronwen, "you are still beset by your horrors and the cold, cold journey and perhaps a touch of poison!" she added, pressing his thigh with a blatant twinkle in her eye, noticed by father and daughter alike as they looked knowingly at each other. Bronwen thought of him as somewhat battle-worn but still very handsome; Inga thought so, too, as she smiled at him.

"We will talk when you are more able!" said Wenslau with a brief grin and headed toward the stables.

Inga couldn't wait; she wanted to know everything about the man, even after Bronwen asked her to desist half a dozen times.

"My name is Grimbald," said the stranger as he settled and hauled himself back to the bed. "Forgive me, I must sleep some more..." He slumped like a dying man onto the temporary bed, knocking over his cup and a small table.

Bronwen said to Inga, "That'll be the 'lixir doing it's trick, so you can ask away. He'll not know you're there, m' girl."

"I haven't heard that name before," said Inga.

"We-l-l-l, I have… but I cannot be sure where," replied Bronwen.

Inga stood over the comatose figure, admiring his rugged appearance, his foreignness. A fascinating man to behold, she thought, and he smelled a little sweeter now.

Shouting and cursing suddenly erupted in the stables, most of it coming from Wenslau. Bronwen and Inga both rushed through to see what was going on, but most of the commotion had finished.

Aedric was standing over young Iain, a servant boy always seemingly suffering mishaps and who appeared to be very clumsy. The boy could hardly walk, but one of Bronwen's maids, Eudda, insisted that Aedric was responsible and said she saw him attempting to slink away just after Iain fell to the floor.

Straight away, Aedric provided a plausible story that his master would probably accept. "I slapped the lad on the head for throwing too much food into the trough for the horses. Maybe I hit him a little too hard, and he was still dazed. You know how clumsy he is, sire!"

"Not an ounce of truth in it!" said Eudda, "He bullies that boy and everyone else when he can."

"Is any of this true?" asked Wenslau, observing the boy's glances.

The boy looked up at Aedric as he looked back with a knowing stare. "N-n-n-o-o," said Iain, "I'm just clumsy, sire," he added unconvincingly.

Wenslau looked questioningly at Aedric's smug face and then at Eudda with her pinched expression. She decided better not to pursue things any further for fear of reprisals.

Unsure of Aedric's behaviour and not for the first time, Wenslau advised Aedric strongly, "Give a little more leeway to the servants, man; I need them fit to do their duties. You were young once and maybe not so clever!"

Aedric certainly did not like the last remark as he stiffened his lips.

Wenslau strode away, thinking how little he needed this kind of trouble when there was so much going on already.

CHAPTER TWO

The Search Party

The next morning, still dark but early, Eudda and another servant girl were busy helping Bronwen pack food and ale for some of the men of the household to go and investigate the previous night's troubles. Eudda related her suspicions about Aedric to Bronwen and a few other problems related to him. The women were chattering away, with their backs to the fire, and then suddenly, they all screamed in shock as Grimbald quietly stood over them, waiting to get a word in.

"Good morning, my lady," he said calmly to Bronwen.

Inga woke bleary-eyed, wiped the sleep from her eyes, and came running in from her room to hear the handsome man speak in his warm, mellow manner. "Might I be so bold as to ask for some food and drink? I can pay."

"Nay… Nay… Nay, sir, I would not hear of such. Please be seated, Mathilda will bring you food and drink quite soon, and payment will NOT be needed," she added with a broad smile.

"Good morning, sir," said Inga with a syrupy sweet grin, "I'm Inga."

"Good morning, child. Yes I remember!" replied Grimbald.

Not liking to be referred to as a child, Inga said. "I'm actually, most nearly a woman thou shouldst know. Of an age to be promised," stated Inga, a little pretentiously.

"Ah, but a girl can be promised at twelve summers old, or even less in many customs Inga!" said Grimbald.

"Well, I am nearly fifteen summers!" stated Inga.

"Nearly fourteen!" interjected Bronwen "… and not a very mature one!" she scoffed. "Now leave the man be, so he can partake of his morning fare."

Grimbald sat and studied his surroundings. He mused how the house was such a melting pot of cultures, with truly little in an orderly fashion, but it had a charm and warmth about it with homely smells. The fire constantly tended, lighting the main room a lovely shade of pale amber. He also found it strange how Wenslau did not advertise himself with a great long house and guards about him.

"I know what you're thinking," said Bronwen, noticing Grimbald looking all about him, "what a strange house we have. Oh, my dearest husband cannot see anything go to waste, so we have a bit of something from everywhere. We could have had his father's long house, but he wanted nothing of it. This is the remains of what was once a roman villa. I had to insist on having these giant flagstones for our floor as my dearest would have had us walking on mud and straw until he could find someone to re-lay a mosaic floor he found in another old Roman villa. I think he still has his intentions on it. He likes what he sees, and tends to have it, no matter what its origin or if it looks well with anything we have already … I despair sometimes," she sighed.

"I sense he's a good man, though, my lady," said Grimbald. "If I may be so bold," he continued, "Why do you work so, my lady? Do you not have enough servants in your household?"

She paused for a few seconds… "Well, my husband and I agreed some time ago after some household thefts and accusations against Aedric, our elder servant, that we would work with the minimum number of people possible… and anyway, I like to work. We all should practice humility, I believe. I like to prepare some of the food we eat, sew some of the clothes, or tend to the animals occasionally. It is what I had been accustomed to as a girl, and I enjoy it. It's what I do that makes me who I am."

Grimbald smiled broadly in admiration, "Such fine sentiments, my lady!" He suddenly turned away, looking towards the rising flames in the fire and subdued burning anger inside. His mind was greatly occupied with the events of the last two days. He had met many challenges, but this was different. He was beset with revenge and loathing like only once before. Feelings he knew he should try to throw off, feelings he was warned not to harbour, and he knew that much of the blame for this dilemma lay with him.

Nothing at this time was much stranger than Loki's odd behavior; a dog who was essentially his own spirit, unattracted to being petted, as Inga would try to do, and never even sitting close to his master. It was as if he could read the mind of the new visitor, and with a show of great empathy, he sat before Grimbald and promptly licked his hands. Grimbald abated his angry thoughts and smiled knowingly at Loki, whereupon the bulky hound curled his body and laid himself at Grimbald's feet.

Bronwen could not believe what she had witnessed, saying that he indeed carried the spirit of nature within him and called to the other women to see this miracle, who were greatly in awe. Inga had retired to her room but came hurriedly back to enquire what the fuss was about, only to find herself standing in silence at the change in her beloved Loki. Wenslau, too, returned from the stables and witnessed the same. Loki raised one eyebrow with a half gaze in his master's direction. Grimbald just smiled at Wenslau like he was an old friend, and Wenslau felt reassured by his new guest.

"Are you well enough to join us, young man? We will be back, I hope, by mid-afternoon. I want to know what occurred last night. I have a fresh horse ready with your weaponry... Lightfoot, he is called, very good with anyone," said the Reeve.

"But husband," protested Bronwen.

"I'll come, sire, but would not fare well in battle!" said Grimbald.

"That is fine with me, young man; we'll watch your back!" replied Wenslau.

A sudden need to visit the toilet became necessary for the new recruit, a combination of trepidation, poisons, and Bronwen's elixir.

"I'll be with you shortly," he said, walking cautiously, hand on stomach, toward the stable and asking the whereabouts of the washroom. Wenslau, laughing at Grimbald's jerky motions, pointed with an open palm.

A large group of men assembled outside Wenslau's house; most were tall and well-built, trained warriors. Wenslau's Huscarls perform various duties, with protecting the village from any outside threat being the most important. They were only a small assembly compared to those that could be mustered. Wenslau was a force to be reckoned with, having almost two hundred fighting men at his immediate disposal. Some of the men, who were more lithe and nimble like Luuah, were on foot. The little Pict was not quite so lithe but a very skilled man in many ways and quick enough. He could track any man or animal in all weather conditions and, along with Loki, was vital in determining the intruders of the previous evening.

Grimbald took to his appointed mount with slight unease, mainly of his condition, only to find his steed was solid and calm, as Wenslau had said. Loki came up alongside Grimbald as if it were his custom to do so.

Wenslau looked down at him with a slight frown and said, "So, you`ve found a new master, eh?"

"Not a new master, sire, just a kindred spirit!" exclaimed Grimbald.

"M-m-mph. You'll ride alongside me; we must talk!" ordered Wenslau as he was mounting. "This is Greymoon. He is six summers of age, has all the ways a fighting horse should have, and we have seen some tussles," he added, making light of his exploits.

Unseen to Grimbald was Inga, surrounded by all the tall figures, but she was a very different creature when scouting with a troupe of men; she was quiet, studious, and alert at all times. Her father gave up a long time ago trying to dissuade her and, suffice to say, saw some element of himself in her young, determined ways.

"Esmond, you will oversee the village. Make yourself available to the wishes of my household," instructed Wenslau to one of his more trusted warriors, as the party rode slowly away.

It wasn't too long before Luuah picked-up signs less than a mile from the village, northeast in the direction of Lord Wealdmaer's land. "These are not the feet of Wealdmaer men, shire!" he said.

"What do you mean?" asked Wenslau.

Grimbald looking on knowingly, interjected. "He means their steps are too erratic, sire, and hurried, with too large a stride for them to be drunk or hunting." His remarks surprised the troupe, whereupon Inga decided to bring her cob a little closer.

"This is where you also came, masser," Luuah said to Grimbald, pointing to a nearby spot. "Dey wrun necksht to hawwshes sho shave time ahh' shnow too deep, would haf made shlow!"

The troupe travelled a few miles further, being careful not to trespass on Wealdmaer's lands. He had made his peace with Wenslau three years ago with a mutual dislike of each other. They would have still been at war if it were not for the intervention of King Aldfrith, an extremely strict ruler and not in the least swayed by the machinations of the Christian autocracy.

The Brigantes and Saxons were now mostly assimilated and were a mighty force and show of power for any king. Aldfrith just needed to ally some of the feuding Northanhymbrians, those loyal to his father but not to him.

Wealdmaer was a sycophant to anyone of greater power or status. He tried to win Aldfrith's trust with little effect, but the King always had a healthy respect for Wenslau. He admired his stubbornness and tenacity and would never see him troubled by any petty squabbles. Added to the fact, Wenslau was decidedly atheistic, in harmony with Osred, Aldfrith's son, who admired Wenslau - a very plus point.

In due time, he would have to honour his ally with more might.

The light that had shone brightly but coldly through the day was now starting to surrender its glow. Wenslau decided to turn back, but one of his scouts, who was further ahead, called his master over with great urgency ... "Here, sire, look!"

"What is that horrible smell?" said Inga hoarsely as Loki trudged through the snow-filled bracken, sniffing furiously.

"I believe that is putrid flesh?" remarked Rowe.

Something was trapped in the hawthorn bush, wrapped in rags, some lost possession? Luuah retrieved it by pushing it through with the aft end of his spear but very gently in case there was something alive. The parcel fell upon the bank of snow beneath the bush and rolled out its contents, to everyone's horror. It was the full arm of a man with recognisable tattoos upon it.

Grimbald's eyes welled up with tears. "Foch, my good friend Uhtric," he tried to stay calm but said with a malevolence in his voice, "FOCHTED SWINE, I WILL SEEK JUSTICE FOR HIM. I WILL BUTCHER THOSE FILTH OF HELL'S DROSS. This matter will be settled by me alone, sire."

"But angry as you may feel, my friend, you are not able and well enough as yet, and I could not see you take on those fetid scum without some help. For now, we must return and prepare for possible battle," insisted Wenslau with conviction.

Luuah picked up the arm, wrapping it in the same cloth, and stated, "I take … find answer," and at that very moment trod in a pile of shit.

Inga straight away said, "That's the smell, ye gods!" Luuah picked up the excrement on a stick and put it in another piece of cloth.

"Dish teww me more!" said Luuah as the troupe returned to their village.

They all turned around and picked up the pace a little to beat the failing light. Pulling on his kit bag, Luuah walked proudly through the snow as if he'd caught some magnificent prey for all to eat, Inga looking on with a disgusted expression. Luuah was a kind little man, always out for the underdog, which was when he was at his fiercest. All his wives were rescued from differing problems, but Fryda was the only one he paid for. His home, an old, dilapidated roman fort house, was a haven to all sorts of animals, many that were runts about to be slaughtered. Unfortunately, he was unable to give them children, but all his wives agreed that is the price of this man's soul they had to forfeit.

CHAPTER THREE

The Journey West

694 AD

Eight years earlier, to the edge of a small hamlet in Southern Saxony, a sinewy, grey-haired, ruddy-faced man scuttled out of his farmhouse to call his family and serfs from the fields and out-buildings for an important meeting. His wife and daughter were tending the geese, cattle, and pigs nearby while his sons were all terribly busy tilling and sowing seeds in the fields, hoping for a better crop for the coming summer.

All seated at a meagre evening meal, the family ate in concentrated silence, trying to savour every mouthful except for Lars, the youngest of the family. Patience was never one of his virtues. He sat with an empty bowl and arms splayed out on the table, asking impudently, "Well, Father, what's the fuss?"

Ulrich, who sat next to Lars, grabbed his arm tightly, looked into his eyes and said, "RESPECT".

Ulrich, the eldest brother, now 18 years old, was dark, tall, strong and wouldn't take any nonsense. Everyone else tolerated Lars because of his sharp wit and entertainment value, but Ulrich was a quiet, serious sort, not easily amused, and ready to discipline his younger brother.

The five brothers plus one sister were getting impatient now, watching their father finish his meal slower than anyone else. As soon as he pushed his empty bowl away, Edwin, the second eldest, begged.

"Father, what is so important; is the country at war with anyone?"

"No, my son, but perhaps at odds with the gods?"

Lars chuckled.

"After these three bad years and the pestilence that followed. We are all lucky to be at this table right now!"

"I didn't feel very lucky with my bowl," chimed Lars.

"Be grateful for what you have… some people are starving in other parts, and many young ones are enslaved without their parents!" said Ulrich.

"M-mm-ph," grunted Lars.

The third youngest brother, Magnus, asked his father, "We're leaving, aren't we?"

Mother was just about to contradict the boy's remark when father raised his hand and said, "Well, I have to ask you all a particularly important question. As you know, my older brother, your uncle Edwin, went to Northanhymbra in Angleland some seven years ago. According to Baldric, the trader, who was there some months ago, he is doing well near the town of Hereteu.

It seems there are more opportunities to trade and farm in Angleland, admittedly, mostly on tied lands, but the majority of landowners are fair, he reported, and I believe the man. He has always traded honestly with us for the tools and everything we've had from him."

Ulrich looked on quizzically.

Father continued, "What I want to know is, which of you would like to come with your mother and me to Angleland? We do not insist that you come. I would respect that you might want to stay here with your Uncle Cedric, who does not want any of us to go. He has the wealth and power enough to keep you all until you are of independent age."

The father, Brodin, and his other elder brother, Cedric, were poles apart. Brodin liked to earn everything through his hard work, but Cedric liked to creep and crawl his way to a position in society. He had adopted Christianity for worldly gains, only to further himself. More than anything, he had such a great need to be popular.

The Christian church at that time was starting to establish small pockets of followers, impressing many with its power, organisation, and wealth. Many Christian scholars had made pilgrimages across northern Europe to try and convert the *Heathen Tribes,* as they called them.

Cedric was an agent and friend of the local Abbot and grew to attain substantial wealth and status through his position. Unfortunately, he had no heirs, and the remainder of his family did not really like him, even his wife. The only member of Brodin's family who liked him a little was Agatha, his niece, a bonny young girl with the whitest of blonde hair and sparkling blue eyes.

"You'll warm the heart of any young man when you're older!" he repeatedly said flatteringly.

He would often present her with small gifts, which annoyed her brothers, especially Lars, her twin brother, who looked nothing like her with his freckles and mop of red hair. Brodin asked Agatha first if she would like to stay with her uncle Cedric who had always doted on her. Cedric liked family company anyway, to show off. Like any girl of her age, Agatha loved the attention and the gifts but was unsure about staying indefinitely with her uncle. None of the boys felt comfortable around Cedric or the company he kept.   So, it was decided the following day that Helga, the mother, would say her goodbyes to her nearby relatives with Agatha and would invite everyone to come that evening for a farewell drink, with what little food they could offer to celebrate their new life.

Helga was always loyal and hard working for her husband and family, but she did not want to leave her parents behind as her sisters did not show affection or respect toward them, even though they had promised to do so. She just could not believe them. Her mother and father were now quite old for their time, in their late fifties and world-weary from a lifetime of hard work, with many trials, tribulations and disappointments. Helga knew this would be the last she would see of them. She wept quietly over several days, remembering how her mother always baked a few loaves each week to help out while her parents had so little themselves. And how her father was always available at harvest or Winterfest for butchering the animals and herding for exchange. They almost came to live with Brodin and his family, but Helga's father was too proud. He always said, "You have your own destinies to fulfil."

Brodin asked the remainder of his family, starting with the youngest boy, before celebrations began.

"Now I want you all to be sure about our quest; Grimbald, what say you?"

"Aye, father, I'll be there at your side!" he said with great affection and unquestioning loyalty.

"Yes, father," came the next two replies.

"Well, my son?" he asked the doubting Ulrich.

"You know I'm not too keen on foreigners, and I still think this area can be worked for profit. The bad weather can't go on, but clearly, you'll need to sell it to go on your way," Ulrich opined.

"I'm sorry, my son, but I will. I have no choice though there may be one option; your two cousins Brandt and Eggbert could help you run the farm, and your uncle Cedric would likely lend the money to keep you until you can repay him unless you can manage with just the servants. I know he would always remind you what he's done, but he has enough heart to oblige. Look for the good in him?" said Brodin.

"A-a-a-ch-ch, father, the last thing I want to do is be indebted to my uncle. I'd never hear the last of it. And those cousins of mine are not the best of workers, particularly Eggbert. But I'm sorry, father, I feel no desire to go to Angleland, and of the Angles I have met, they are an arrogant sort," stated Ulrich.

"Did he say he does not like foreigners … how about the way he drools over that Romanisch girl at the Goera market?" observed Lars.

Ulrich glowered.

"That's enough," said Helga, "we must all be civil to one another, especially now!"

Lars smiled cheekily at his eldest brother.

The evening went well as they spent the time with their relatives, with tears, tales, antics and laughter; a lot of the latter was provided by Lars, who tried dressing up like his uncle Cedric and made sarcastic remarks. Good thing Cedric had gone when he did.

"I am summoned for Papal business!" said Cedric making his case to leave early and sincerely wishing Brodin's family luck. "Good luck, and may God go with you!" he said with a little tear welling in his eye.

Not long afterwards, Helga's mother and father left, and for the first time she could remember, tears started to brim her father's eyes. There was always something special in him that she could not quite fathom.

Lars had been looking out of the window to watch his uncle leave, after which he quickly dressed in pretend finery from his mother's ceremonial clothes and strutted through the room, wafting his hand through the air, bellowing, "Papal business, you know? Must go; good luck, peasants." And then wiping away a gush of pretend tears.

Brodin looked on disappointedly, but everyone else was amused, even Ulrich!

Lars did what he did best and made light of the occasion, which pleased his mother in a way, as her sadness was sapping her enthusiasm for the venture and validating her husband's hopes for a better future. Brodin had provisionally sold most of his stock and land against his better judgement to Lord Aethelric of Higher Friedland, a powerful man but still a pagan. Although the price could have been better, he accepted but only on special terms, in the proviso that Ulrich was not to take on the farm.

Both fortunately and unfortunately, the Reeve was not too pleased when Brodin later informed Lord Aethelric that his son Ulrich had decided to run the farm with Cedric's money and hired help, in Cedric's name, of course. If it were not for the power of the local Abbot, small as it was, events could have been dire for Ulrich and Cedric. Many Saxon mercenaries were now on the payroll of the Christian church and able to offer protection to loyal subjects. As showy as he was, he promised Ulrich, "We will be attentive to your security!" and despite his braggartly ways, Cedric truly meant what he said.

CHAPTER FOUR

Harald Goodman

Three days after Brodin's announcement, the family were all on their way, with some livestock, having sold the cattle to his brother, who would, in turn, give them back to Ulrich. Everyone was incredibly nervous, but most were excited about their venture. They had just five pigs, twelve geese, twenty bags of seed, eight sacks of roots and animal feed, food, and ale of their own, as well as some blankets for the ten-day journey, which were handily packed. They had one big wagon for themselves and one small cart tied to the back for the geese to stay in at night. The pigs would walk, tied together behind that, overlooked by Edwin or Magnus.

Brodin hid his money carefully in the false bottom of a small feeding trough for the pigs, making sure Lars did not know in case he somehow blurted it out. Then he filled his purse to a suitable level. Grimbald saw everything. Unbeknown to his father; like Edwin, Grimbald didn't miss much. Magnus, often bored, would taunt the geese rather persistently while Edwin was on constant vigil over all passers-by.

It was on day four that Edwin alerted his family as they approached the brow of a hill, where they would meet some unsavoury company. Certain events went awry as some Thuringian mercenaries were returning home from a borderland battle with a Frankish tribe. They were not bothered whether anyone gave food and ale freely or they had to take it. Their leader asked in a menacing way if Brodin could spare a couple of geese, some bread and ale, to which Brodin replied politely, "Yes, well, I can spare our largest goose, but we can spare no more as we are on our way to Angleland, we need all the provisions we can muster for ourselves."

It was all Lars could do to contain himself as the leader agreed to the offer, looking the family over with great scrutiny. For once, Lars kept his mouth closed but looked on impudently. The leader remarked and glared at Lars, "That gingery boy needs to learn some manners. He's a danger to himself," as he bagged one of the geese and another took some bread and ale from Helga. "Angleland, you say, good luck there then, you'll need it!" said the man sneeringly.

Lars threw his fist at them as they went out of sight, still trembling, having had his taste of real fear. The afternoon air was cold though the sun shone brightly. They made their way to the next small town, which could be detected by the smell of food, smoke, and livestock.

Gottingen was a fairly new stronghold for a garrison of Christian soldiers with quite a good trading market, and Brodin had a cousin there he had not seen for many years, who could maybe provide shelter for part of their journey. They'd had two nights in the woods. Some of the bears were out of hibernation, and wolves were plenty in those parts, which could make things extremely uncomfortable as they would have to move their camp if the wind changed. Other travellers could also pose problems. It was either Edwin or Brodin that kept a vigil at night, constantly keeping a fire going.

Brodin decided he'd need to buy a big enough cart to carry all the livestock; he didn't want the pigs to lose fat. Grimbald and Magnus would manage the third cart, so Lars and Agatha would be asked to keep an eye on the geese. This would help them make better headway for Nijmegen.
Brodin was trying to balance the books between how much they would need for provisions, the transportation cost to Angleland and how much they might need when they got there if everything Baldric had told them was true.

Daylight was starting to give way to night as the weary family trundled into Gottingen. Soldiers, the epitome of any Saxon warrior with neat hair and clothing, shining metal buckles and studs, roamed the streets in small groups or pairs, watching everyone coming and going. Edwin was tired, Lars was kicking stones, Magnus was playing his pipe whistle softly, and Grimbald was just looking at the sky, hands behind head, from the back of the goose cart, daydreaming.

Without noticing, two men startled everyone, including the pigs and geese, as they appeared from the left of the wagon out of a small street.

"Halt!" one of the men ordered, "What is your business here?"

Brodin told the men who he was and was looking for his cousin and family.

"Oh-h-h, Harald Goodman, we call him." The soldier responded after a moment's thought and indicated where Harald's house was. "About seven hundred paces to the right from Kirk Strasse on the right. Just a tad down the side from the Inn!"

Looking from the road, as they came near to Harald's house, was the Inn, where soldiers were drinking, eating, and cavorting with local women with much bare flesh on display. Only Ulrich had ever seen such activities, but the rest of the brothers were totally innocent to town life, as was Agatha and her mother, except for the occasional visit to the market. Lars was taking full note for future antics.

Grimbald and Magnus didn't know what to make of it all, but Edwin wanted to be a part of it. He wanted to be a Saxon warrior, even if it meant being a proper Christian like his mother and father. Brodin and Helga disapproved of the revelries but only in a token Christian fashion. They were just really being healthy men and women, in their eyes.

A few moments later, on their journey, Edwin spotted the house set well back from the road with large cattle grazing in a walled field in front. There were many people walking about to the side of the huge farmhouse, light glowing through half-closed wooden shutters with their waxed hessian screens. At the gate was a well-set, cheerful-looking man with long brown, finely plaited hair and a beard going grey at the tips. He was talking and laughing with another man at the gate when he caught sight of the entourage looking tired and travel-weary.

Harald had not seen Brodin since they were both young single men. He was then a slender wispy bearded young man and well-liked by everyone, especially the ladies. The glint and charms of the man were still there, and Brodin recognised him almost immediately despite his embodiment of good living. Brodin reminded Harald who he was and, with a little hesitation, saw the older version of his once favourite cousin. The two greeted each other very heartily, slapping each other on the back like they were still young and full of vigour. Harald mocked Brodin for his grey locks while smiling his charming smile at Helga, with a little wink for Agatha. Brodin, in turn, mocked Harald for his paunch.

The whole family were endeared and welcomed into Harald's household and were given the special servants' quarters. But Harald made sure his servants were also rewarded for their sacrifice, living up to the name he was given by the town. Brodin and his family were treated like royalty. They had never seen so much food, ale, wine, and mead flow in one place and at one enormous table.   All, having said grace, were quiet and polite as the family tucked into the great spread.

Harald was a man used to entertaining and lived life to the full.

"What is mine is yours," he would say. "Take your fill; ask, and it is yours … if I still have it … Ha-Ha-HA?"

Brodin's prayers were about to be answered in more ways than he would ever have dreamt. Fortune seemed to have smiled on Brodin and his family after many years. All slept well that night, especially Lars, who got quite drunk.

The next morning there was heavy rain. There were people all over the place getting the cattle and fowl undercover. Despite his volume of ale the previous night, Harald had been up since the crack of dawn organising the work schedule. Brodin walked up to Harald in the yard later as if there was nothing inclement about the weather and complimented him on his magnificent farm and business. They both spent a long time together that morning, Brodin helping as they spoke about all the aspects of their work. It was almost as if they had gone back in time with that strong family bond that so many Saxons shared.

Harald had to remind Brodin a few times not to do the chores of a servant.

"They wouldn't like it, you know. You'll put them out of work!" he jested.

At mid-morning, a loud call from an extra-large cowbell rang for all to come to breakfast. Harald's family was quite large, but all his children were girls, something Agatha was quite pleased about. As they sat at the breakfast table, some of Harald's daughters started smiling and teasing Lars about his bright red hair, which riled him. So, he decided to give them something to think about. Something Lars could almost do on demand was a fart. He gave one of the loudest, longest farts in Saxony, with a bright red face and smiling impishly at the girls. All the children started laughing, and a couple of the servants cramped a smile. Startlingly and most unexpectedly, Harald rose out of his chair, picked Lars up by the scruff of his neck like he weighed nothing, and smacked him hard across the head, almost knocking him unconscious. Brodin and Helga were shocked, she wanted to say something, but Brodin grabbed her arm. They knew they had been too lenient with Lars.

"You are going to have breakfast with the pigs, young man; nobody disrespects my family or his own at my table." Lars started to struggle, with tears in his eyes. He wasn't used to such harsh discipline. Harald's daughters watched on in horror.

"If you don't want another welt, you'll be still. Take him to the pigsty," he ordered one of his manservants. "You've been too soft with that lad. He'll be the death of you if you're not careful," said Harald to Brodin and Helga as he walked calmly back to his seat.

Lars was escorted to the pigsty and given gruel to eat from a bowl which was strung up away from the pigs. He was warned not to come out of the sty until Harald said so, or his punishment would be more embarrassing and painful than he could imagine.

Back at the breakfast table, Harald was detailing what he could provide Brodin and family with for the remainder of their journey and asked when they wished to leave. "You are most welcome to stay, cousin. I know I have my ways, and you have yours, but there is always room for some compromise. We should all strive to make this life a happy one. If you <u>are</u> determined to emigrate, though, cousin, may I make one small request?"

"Anything Harald, my god, after all your generosity, I could not think to decline," replied Brodin.

"Well, I have these two servants, for lack of a better title, more like friends… They are brother and sister who we rescued from slavery some years ago. She has ways about her that are quite different, but good ways. They are Parisi by birth but lived most of their lives in Mercia, in Angleland, where their father was from, it's a long story. They have a very chequered history, but they would both be of great asset to you, Brodin and Helga. If you could take them a part way? And another little word of advice, see if you can culture trade with the church when you settle. It has paid dividends for me."

Brodin raised his eyebrows and nodded in silence.

After breakfast, all the children went to see how Lars was taking his punishment. Grimbald and Edwin knew he would turn things around. Magnus thought he might be sulking, but just as true to form, Lars had taken off all his clothes, daubed himself all over in the mud, fashioned a leather pouch to look like a pig's snout, added floppy pieces of cloth for ears, and a curled twig strapped on him to look like a pig's tail. He was crawling around the pen and squealing a mock scream of a pig, with occasional grunting, causing the whole farmyard to erupt in laughter.

Agatha wet herself laughing at her outrageous brother. Unfortunately for Lars, events didn't quite go as he had planned. In fact, they quite literally came to bite him on the bum. One of the elder sows did not take kindly to his antics and subsequently sank her teeth into his muddied left buttock, which caused even more people to flock and laugh at Lars' buffoonery. By now, everyone from the breakfast table was about and laughing hysterically to see Lars hopping about in his silly props, holding his left butt in search of a cool watering hole to soothe his tender wound.

"I hope you're going to apologise to our Tilda for upsetting her and her sisters," said the swineherd to Lars sarcastically, stifling his own laughter as Lars quickly dipped his bottom into a water trough, rubbing away at the pain.

Brodin and his family all joined in the day's chores, including Lars, though on lighter duties because of his wound. *Punishment exacted,* thought Harald.

By midday, servants were sent to help Brodin and Helga prepare for their journey the following morning. Harald's wife, Aenid, who was a noticeably quiet and shy woman and had hardly spoken during their stay, came up to the pair and said, "Good day, Brodin and Helga. I'd like to introduce you to your journey companions to Angleland.

They are lovely loyal friends as well as nice people. We will miss them dearly!"

She waved her hand back, and a few paces behind were these two tall, olive-skinned, dark-haired individuals with friendly, smiling faces. From behind her mother's skirt, Agatha looked on warily, saying nothing as usual. The brother was quite broad in the shoulders and an athletic-looking sort. The sister, equally athletic in appearance but slimmer, had a kind of confident demeanour, a handsome woman. The man greeted Brodin, "Good day, sir, my name is Gris, and this is my sister, Myrte. I am a metal smith, and my sister is a diviner and medicine woman."

Brodin gulped with surprise.

"She is also a fine warrior!" he added.

"As are you, brother," his sister interjected.

"I hope we will be of some value and assistance to you and your family, sir. We are most grateful to accompany you on your venture. Alas, we must go home to find out what has become of our father and our family," said Gris rather sadly.

Helga smiled broadly at the couple and then at Brodin.

"All is settled then?" said Aenid.

"Aye... to you and my cousin, I am indebted. Proud of you all, and for this couple... I wish to help them as you have helped me. I feel as if I am learning so much more about life and, at my age, how fine it can be!" Brodin remarked, with a little tear forming in the corner of his eye and slightly hung over from the night before.

Brother and sister smiled again at each other and at their new hosts. It was a knowing smile, a sort of told-you-so look.

CHAPTER FIVE

Watered and Renewed

The next morning Brodin and his family made arrangements for their journey. They got a newer, bigger wagon for themselves and a larger cart for the livestock and extra provisions for their sea voyage. The two horses which they left home with had been well-fed and watered; they were ready for the journey with a renewed vigour in their steps. Harald gifted a horse to pull the second cart, enabling them to move faster and gain more ground.

Coming alongside the family's wagon were two large pack horses, heavily laden and mounted by Gris and Myrte. Gris said to Brodin and Helga, "We will follow behind, sir, as thieves would be more likely to come from the rear to steal your animals before attempting anything else."

Brodin nodded and agreed, feeling he was in good hands. Harald and Aenid wished the family well and offered them to come back any time they wished.

As things turned out, most of the remaining journey was relatively uneventful except for one close call and a very strange encounter with a band of gypsies. It started as merely an argument over who had killed their wild boar for supper, which got out of hand.

Edwin had shot the animal with his arrow. It was only wounded when one of the gypsies speared to finish it off and carry it away. Edwin protested to the man that it was his quarry. Magnus and Grimbald were alongside Myrte. Gris, who was a short distance away in the forest, had witnessed what happened.

Myrte was wearing her bow and ran a few strides from the opportunist, suggesting he give up his ill-gotten gains. The man laughed and sneered, carrying on hauling the carcass. Gris was behind her, looking around to make sure no one else would intervene. She put an arrow to her bow as quickly as a flea.

Edwin shouted, "It doesn't matter".

It was too late!

Edwin, Grimbald, and Magnus soon witnessed the fury and temper of Myrte. Magnus was quite afraid, but Grimbald was transfixed. He felt an awe-inspired faith in Myrte. Agatha was also in awe as she watched from a distance.

The thief did not get far as an almighty burning pain entered his right thigh; he fell straight to the ground in agony. Myrte removed the spear from the carcass and plunged it into the ground within an inch of the man's face, staring at him as he writhed in agony.

She stood over the man and dragged hold of the prize, calmly saying to him, "Tell your people what you have done and why you are here like this when they find you. DO NOT LIE."

Myrte then walked away, supremely confident, not even looking behind her. Magnus and Edwin were shocked; Grimbald grinned and then coughed with excitement.

The family settled back together. Everyone got busy with the chores allocated to them, feeding and watering the animals and turning the feed, so it did not go mouldy. Calming the geese was not easy in the woods with so many predators. They were also too slow on their travels. The pigs were alright. Initially running behind, but soon caught up. Brodin didn't want them to lose weight for the market. The journey was not easy.

Just as Myrte was loading the boar onto the large trellis for butchering near the wagon, Edwin, ever on the lookout, called out, "Everyone, those people... they're coming here for us, LOOK!"

Myrte and Gris were not surprised one bit as they turned to face the party. The group of ten visitors was led by a tall, fat, and ugly woman with thinning black curly hair.

"She looks as fierce as she looks ugly!" said Lars, "I'd bet her porridge goes sour soon as she looks at it!" he added loudly.

"Shut up!" ordered Edwin.

The woman's voice matched her appearance as she growled at Myrte in a stilted Germanic accent. "Dat was you hurt my boy, yah? You tough lady, ehh? You give back boar and we have reward, too, so none of you get hurt, eh?" she said menacingly.

Eight men and one other woman were in the posse, all looking in various states of ugliness and aggression.

Myrte replied calmly and confidently, "Do you want to die today or leave it until it comes to you naturally? That goes for the rest of you," she added more loudly.

The ugly woman looked with bewilderment at Myrte, coolly holding her sword, while Gris looked on malevolently at the woman with his hand on the hilt of his sword.

As she was about to summon her bloodthirsty squad, a second glance from the woman informed her of how terribly wrong she might be in challenging Myrte's words. A glint of something worn beneath Myrte's sleeve, which she had only seen once before, brought back a distant memory and signified a sudden sense of terror.

"We go back, hurry, hurry!" she said, not daring to venture any further. She ordered her party to return in their own language, saying they would not gain much by challenging the Brodin family. Not one of the ugly woman's people would ever question her, for hers was the last word!

That same evening was as peaceful as they could ever have wished. There was a slight breeze with lovely wafts of wild flora and fauna from the forest. The fire also glowed steadily and soothingly throughout the night.

Grimbald was unable to sleep and offered to keep watching when Edwin retired, so their father could get more sleep.

Helga was up late as usual, washing pots, bowls, spoons, and knives, cleaning the spit, portioning, and wrapping the meat for the next day. Myrte looked at Helga before retiring and asked rather feebly if she could help. Helga, who recognised that Myrte was no domestic goddess, declined her offer with thanks.

As the party was nearing the end of their journey, the countryside suddenly opened up into huge, organised fields with healthy crops and noble-looking buildings with the recognisable aromas of the farmyard.

CHAPTER SIX

The Crossing

The road leading to Nijmegen was a busy one, with so many types of traders having a wide variety of shops. People were milling about every which way. Brodin and his family were mesmerised by how busy and how many people were in one place. Along the quayside were half-mile queues of wagons leading up to the jetty. Animals, horsemen, and mules were all waiting for their turn to board the big boats.

Myrte said to Brodin, "It's up to you, sir, but some of the boat masters charge a lot of money to take carthorses across the sea as they do not travel well. If you want to wait for a cheaper vessel, we might have to stay a few more days; it can get dangerous at night. I would say sell the horses you have and use our horses to pull the wagon and cart when we get across until you find some more to buy."

Brodin and Helga looked at each other questioningly. "I am reluctant to sell my faithful friends, lady, but if we can do as you say, then that is what I shall do. Do you know of anyone that would buy and care for them?" asked Brodin.

"I will know soon enough," Myrte said as she walked off to survey the dockside area. "Are you coming, brother? she added.

"Shall we wait here on the green, mistress, or the quayside?" enquired Brodin.

"Please call me Myrte... and yes, wait there," she replied as Gris went over to join her.

Grimbald was besotted with this woman, so brave and so mysterious. Magnus could see how his brother was becoming enchanted and started to tease. "She's old enough to be our mother, Grim. You must be crazy... she's crazy."

"Hush, not so loud I don't want Lars blethering on about it all the voyage. He just doesn't know when to stop," said Grimbald.

Agatha giggled, listening in. Grimbald gave her one of his looks.

Edwin was getting a little impatient, looking for suspicious characters, which were many, all the time. "I'm going to see what we have to do to get on the ship. The sooner we get away from here, the better."

"Don't be too long," said Helga, "we might have to move the wagon with all these people coming in."

He had been away for nearly an hour, and the family was getting worried, especially as Myrte and Gris had not returned either. Shortly, Myrte and Edwin appeared around the side of a covered wagon, as reported by Magnus.

Myrte shouted, "Not to worry, all is settled. We sail tonight. The weather is said to be fair, but there is much to do. We found a buyer for your horses on a farm nearby!"

Edwin interjected, "Yes, I overheard a man from the port saying he wanted some horses. He was arguing with the farmer for not being able to get them cheaper anywhere. I knew you would not be happy with a lower price, father; at least you'd know where they were going."

Myrte interrupted, "Yes. I think you have raised quite a businessman here! He told the man how much he would sell the horses for, which the man accepted right away. We must unhitch and deliver them now as we have made a bargain with one of the captains. That space you see there is ours to fill, and we must be there promptly. Ahhh, here is my brother!"

Coming casually away from the quayside, Gris waved and suddenly broke into a light trot, realising the urgency of the moment. "Good news, we are sailing at the first tide.

The weather is decidedly in our favour, partly due to the waning of the moon, as the captain said, and you could take your horses if you wish for five gelds extra."

"Yes, I informed them of the weather, but we have sold the horses and will buy more when we get to Angleland," Myrte said.

Brodin felt quite out of his depth and asked how much in total for the crossing. He worried whether he would have enough money left to establish themselves when they reached their destination. So many things to think about, much of what was happening started to swamp him.

Helga picked up on his anxiety and suggested, "It's not too late to turn back, my husband. We were welcome to go back to your cousin's home. I would not be disappointed in you, you know?"

"No, my dear, you know my mind is never to go back once a mission is undertaken. The crossing is twelve geld and five pieces. We will sell the horses as first decided; at least they are likely to be going to a worthy home, I hope," Brodin said with resolve.

"I think that is wise," added Gris with a nod of approval from Myrte.

Grimbald stared at Myrte fascinatedly but suddenly saw her stare at her brother Gris with a worrying look. Her actions disturbed Grimbald as she looked like someone overwhelmed by sadness. Her head was down and was silent while helping Gris and Brodin unhitch the horses.

Then very quickly, she tethered them together, mounted her own horse, wrapped the rope to her saddle, and rode off with them stumbling behind.

The horses were sold, and Myrte promptly pocketed the money for Brodin. She was still looking quite sorrowful as Grimbald watched her return. Gris noticed Grimbald's fascination and smiled to himself. As an afterthought, he recalled what Myrte said to him when they were about to leave Harald's farm, which he surmised, must concern Grimbald.

Myrte returned less than an hour later and presented a small purse of money to Brodin. "The farmer has paid a little extra as he hasn't seen such well-kept horses for many a day! He was well pleased and promised they were going to be well cared for again, and I do not doubt him," she assured.
Brodin smiled with a great sense of comfort.

Soon they were in the queue waiting to board the ship; they were second in turn with Gris and Myrte.

One of the crews from the ship came up to the family and said in a Nederlander accent, sounding official, "When you are aboard, we load the animals and fowl first, then the horses go in the hold. Once your wagon is in place, prepare to remove the wheels and place them in the wagon securely, we will help if need be. If the weather turns against us, you can shelter with the animals, otherwise, stay in your wagon or under canvas. We will arrive in Hereteu in three days, all being well. Anyone travelling on to

Whitby will have to wait another day or more if you stay on this ship."

The ship was huge with steep sides, built like a Roman cargo ship. It was quite dark in places and smelled of a variety of things, some, none too pleasant. The front part of the ship had a deck above the hold and gangways on either side, running all the way to the aft end.

It could only carry five medium-sized wagons at one time, so Brodin had to pay extra silver to have the extra wagon for his animals. The journey became slightly more expensive than he bargained for, but after selling the horses, things evened out.

Edwin noticed a name on the side as they boarded; it was called 'The Merman'. In the middle was a kind of kitchen with a fire made from a basket of heavy metal bars containing a circle of stones. The animal hold was probably the cleanest place of all as it had been newly swilled and cleaned with fresh straw in place, and an attendant crew member held a lantern on a pole for everyone to see where to put their livestock and horses. The full organisation of boarding the ship impressed the whole family, and they were soon in place to sit and eat their evening meal.

The ship was about to set sail when the captain bellowed, "For all our safety, no one is to cook, no fires, all forbidden. If you want to cook any meat, fish, or vegetables, bring it in turn to my cooks and they will see to your food."

"That man looks mean!" remarked Agatha to the family.

Luckily, Helga had made some broth earlier, and they had a good supply of bread with dried salted meat, courtesy of Harald's cook.

Gris and Myrte were now both happy to join the family in their first meal aboard ship on their journey to a new life. Lars had been well-behaved until now but started to get restless, thinking he could play mocking games with the crew. Gris went up to him and warned him that if he wasn't careful, they wouldn't think twice about throwing him overboard. Lars didn't know any better but thought it a possibility, so decided to behave for the rest of the journey, at least with everyone except the family.

Most of the children liked to look over the sides at sea and the land they were leaving, as did some adults. Magnus spotted a girl with another family he had taken a shine to. She also noticed him as they exchanged glances and smiled at each other.

Helga wasn't taking the voyage too well as she suffered from seasickness. Myrte soon came to her aid and gave her an elixir that took away the sickness but made her a little giggly. She had never felt this good in her life. Brodin became a little concerned and asked if she was going to be alright.

"She'll be fine, sir. The full strength will wear off soon, and she should be able to travel peacefully from here on," insisted Myrte.

On the second evening of the voyage, for some reason, Grimbald could not sleep. He knew he'd had a bad dream but couldn't remember it clearly. He had such mixed feelings now about their destination. As he stood on the upper deck, Myrte came alongside him. The half-moon's shimmer was dancing across the water and onto their faces as they looked over the empty sea. A soft green glow flitted behind the clouds. The young lad started to feel more relaxed in her company and not so infatuated anymore.

"Grimbald, I have something to tell you that I want you to remember," she began as Grimbald started to feel nervous, not sure what she was about to say.

Myrte continued, "There will come a terrible time in the not-too-distant future when you will want to scream and cry out for every good reason. A time you will want to follow someone, but for the good of yourself and many more people, you must do neither. Help will come to you. Some time from now, you will go on an epic journey, a lone journey. You will be tutored by someone with great gifts and talents. I shall envy you for that privilege. But once he says you are to leave him, you must do exactly as he says. Promise me you will remember this."

Grimbald was just about to question everything Myrte said when there was a sudden cry from the forward end of the ship.

"BELAY... BRIGANDS! BE ABOUT MEN, TO THE PORTSIDE!" A frenzy of the crew came from seemingly nowhere, armed to the teeth and pushing everyone aside to be on the deck, ready to fight. "BE AT ARMS AND READY TO BATTLE!" cried the lookout.

Gris came up to join Myrte, knowing well that she would not be shy of battle. He had his hand on his sword, willing to do the same.

The longship was almost upon them. Her crew was getting ready to set light to their arrows, but Myrte was ahead of their game. She swiftly took oil and flame from the cook's range and let loose a burning arrow into their lead bowmen's skull. She continued firing into the vessel, releasing seven flamed arrows at them. The crew of 'The Merman' could not believe their eyes; she had single-handedly scuppered the raiding party who were now jumping overboard to escape the flames. Many of the pirates were burning alive as they leapt into the water. Passengers were all vying to see the activities. The captain of 'The Merman' told Myrte and company, "Maybe now, those Norse raiders will think twice about taking our ships and goods."

Most of the passengers on board were ignorant of the fact that occasional pirates would take people for slaves or worse, along with their worldly possessions. It was not good for business to tell people about the dangers of crossing the German Sea.

Many were afraid and started chattering amongst themselves. Although Myrte was the heroine of the hour, some were suspicious of her, particularly as she always wore black or dark clothing and carried a bow across her back most of the time. It was obvious; she was nobody's wife or servant, and tongues would wag at what she might be. Gris also used to wear a range of dark clothing but exuded a sense of sophistication and always seemed to allay people's concerns over his sister, a man of cool charm. On this occasion, though, he had his work cut out.

Love seemed to blossom for Magnus and his new girlfriend, but it was fleeting as the journey was about to end; the Hereteu port was in their sight. Brief as it was, the two managed to kiss, hoping to meet again someday, then reluctantly returned to their families. The ship had to wait a couple of hours to dock, allowing Myrte another opportunity to talk to take Grimbald.

"Don't forget what I said earlier, Grimbald... and tell no one about this!" she insisted. One thing Grimbald was exceptionally good at was keeping a secret.

Agatha had watched Myrte talking confidentially to her brother and decided to ask him about it later.

"HAVE YOUR HORSES AND WAGONS READY!" shouted the captain as the pilot boat brought the ship to dock.
Brodin went to check the pigs' trough for the umpteenth time to make sure his stash was still safe.

"I'm sure it is still all there, my dear, unless you've worried it away," mused Helga as she packed for the next phase of their journey.

The port was much smaller than Rotterdam, but it was extremely busy. There was a strong smell of fish due to the amount of small fishing boats hauled up along the beach. They would swiftly unload their catch to a merchant and return to sea on the full tide so as to make the most of the day. Soon the guttural voices of the dockers broke out, giving orders to the pilot of their incoming ship. It was a strange mix of Saxon and Schottish, as they had been told.

The noise of the dropping sails was deafening and frightened the animals as they neared the quayside. Soon the animals and wagons were organised into their prospective parties to be hoisted by a large wooden crane onto the quay. Gris and Myrte tethered their horses to the wagons to get the family away from the harbour.

"GOOD LUCK ON YOUR VENTURE!" shouted the Captain to Myrte and family, "and I thank thee for thy help," he added, pressing a purse into her hand.

Myrte smiled at the man and said, "Be extra careful for now, sir. I may have disturbed a hornet's nest!"

The captain gave a pinched expression and nodded as he returned to his duties.

Hereteu was a small town to behold with an enormous wooden enclosure. Passengers started to disembark. The small town was full of people like Rotterdam but more congested, smelly, and remarkably busy.

CHAPTER SEVEN

Hereteu

Looking about their destination, they observed a large half-stone, half-wooden abbey and a tall church that seemed to have quite an influence over the town, having many monks and nuns doing business with the residents. It was so different a place to back home in Saxony.

The family slowly made their way across the marshy causeway, meeting many locals as they passed; they were uplifted by how friendly the people were. Understanding them, though, was a different matter. The sun was glinting through clouds, and a warm breeze wafted off the land with the more familiar scent of farm and livestock. To the south was a mass of red stone cliffs with sand dunes, scattered houses, boats, and a parcel of trees. Westerly, were green hills and scattered forests. To the north, dark cliffs and wild-looking woodland.

Gris said suddenly, "I had spoken to one of the crew earlier, who told me where we would get horses at a good price. I believe it is just a few miles south of here, Stoctun on the River Teihs; I believe it is called. We should get there before nightfall."

"Is that the place where your brother lives?" Helga asked.

Brodin nodded his head, "I think so."

Everyone was incredibly quiet, even Lars, as they were tired from their journey. Their baby sister had slept most of the way.

Myrte looked at her brother with sadness, which he knew, was related to the family. "This is so hard," she whispered.

"I know, sister, but you are best made to do it! This is a shame you are not so able to open the veils of our future," replied Gris.

As the night sky dimmed, Gris asked around for Brodin's brother. He eventually found someone whom he could communicate with and help him in his search. So, they all decided to look for fresh horses in the morning and seek sanctuary at Edwin's farm.

The road leading to Edwin's farm, was a winding track through large mature horse chestnut and sycamore trees with the occasional ash and elm. At the top of a gently sloping bank was the address described, with low growing hedgerow. There were many cattle wandering about, and it looked like a wealthy farmstead. Gris enquired when two young men and an older woman came to the gate, armed to the hilt with spear, axe, and sword.

"Who are you?" asked the woman rather aggressively.

"I am Brodin of Goera; come to seek out my brother Edwin. Is this his place?" replied Brodin.

"By the gods, mother, it's uncle Brodin!" exclaimed the younger of the two men.

"I'm afraid to tell, he is no longer with us," said the woman and started crying as the elder man put his arm around her.

"Mother, please go inside. We'll talk with the uncle and his family. Take her to the house," he said to one of the servants who had just come across the fields.

I am Bada, and this is my brother Eadberht; we are your nephews. I don't know if you remember us. As you know, our mother died giving birth to Eadberht, but Ebba is every bit our mother now. Alas, if you had been here; two months ago, you would have found father alive and well..."

"Oh my god! I was so looking forward to meeting my brother and a true friend Edwin..." wept Brodin, Helga's eyes welling with tears also. He continued, still sobbing slightly, "Aye, it was the loss of your mother and all those years without a wife that prompted your father to come here, and he must have felt you needed another mother. We often talked of it before he left. And I would never have recognised either of you if I passed you in the field... but you, Eadberht, you do have a slight look of Wassa, your mother."

Eadberht looked a little lost for words; Agatha broke the ice by striking up a conversation, then Lars and Magnus joined in. Edwin, meanwhile, had gone to the rear wagon to feed the pigs and geese.

Gris and Myrte suggested they might go to find lodgings in Stoctun, but Bada said there would be ample room for everyone.

Brodin apologised and asked Bada to continue. "It was one very calm, warm evening, just turned dark, and we heard the cattle rustling and seemed frightened by something. Father insisted we stay at supper while he tended to them. We heard a sudden call as he told something or someone to get out... there was a loud bang, so we dashed out only to find father lying on the floor of the byre, trampled and bloodied by the beasts. He never woke from that time and died a few days later."

Gris asked why they produced arms at the gate and looked ready to battle. Badda promised an explanation when they came to the table after settling in!

The whole family, Gris, Myrte, and Ebba with the two sons sat at the table, slightly uncomfortable at first, but after a couple of ales and some local wine from the abbey, everyone started to relax.

"I'm sorry to ask, Ebba," said Helga quietly as they sat together, "but why did you not have any more children with your husband?"

Myrte looked down at the table pensively and slightly annoyed by that all too common enquiry. *As if all women should be made to produce offspring to justify their place in the world,* she thought. Helga was a very pleasant soul but somewhat annoying to Myrte with her wifey ways.

Ebba answered slowly, "We tried many times, but none would stay in my body. I was quite ill many times with a great loss of blood. I'm afraid God would not allow me that comfort and destiny."

Helga warmed Ebba with sympathy. She was feeling increasingly comfortable in Ebba's company after discovering she was also Christian. She then offered to go outside and talk more about womanly things. As they left the table, Helga looked in Myrte's direction, who returned a quick half smile as if to say not to bother asking, Helga, all the while, knowing the answer.

"You were going to tell us why you were armed so preparedly for battle," reminded Brodin.

Magnus interrupted to ask where he could go for a pee, as he and Lars both had drunk too much ale.

"I'm coming too," said Lars, slurring his words and looking very much the worse for wear. As much as he would like to have grabbed the spear by the door for a play fight with Magnus, Lars had started to learn a little more respect for other people after his incident in the woods with the Thuringian soldiers. Apart from that, he was too intoxicated to do much at all; in fact, the contents of his stomach erupted just outside the house on his way to the toilet. Lars had never suffered quite so badly for his indulgences before and, like many, swore never to do it again. He was having some adventures for an eleven-year-old boy. All the host family liked Lars; he was a breath of fresh air with his cheekiness and antics.

Ebba wanted everyone to join them at church for the service in Hereteu, so she invited Brodin to stay until the following Sunday. Ebba proudly described how they would soon have a church in Stoctun on the Teihs. Ebba asked everyone who would like to join her at church. Eadberht opted to stay at the farm, as did Magnus and Grimbald.

"Lars can stay also if you would like," offered Eadberht.

Gris and Myrte said they would help to keep an eye on things also. They actually had other plans, less hands-on, but for fulfilling a part of their quest.

64

CHAPTER EIGHT

In His Namesake

Edwin had taken great interest in how the farm was managed and got on well with his cousins. He was sixteen years old, a conscientious worker, and a worthy asset to Ebba and her family. He knew father would be upset but asked, not anticipating either way, if he could stay with his cousins and help in their business.

"My son, I had half expected you to say just this, seeing how well you are doing here and much. As I could do with your help in our future venture, I think maybe your brothers and sister will make up the difference," said Brodin unconvincingly. "Anyway, it would be providence you should follow in your uncle's name. They certainly have some good breeds of cattle in this country. I believe there are some real opportunities here in Angleland," he added.

"Many, many thanks, father, this means so much... you know I could still visit. At least we are in the same country. You could send a word when you have found a new homestead, and I could come to visit you," said Edwin trying to reassure his father.

Agatha had always looked up to Edwin and begged him to come with them, but he insisted on staying and told her he would not visit soon.

It was on the misty, murky Sunday morning, Myrte decided to consult her spiritual advisers. For her, there was no better place than an open woodland which was just a stone's throw from the farm. As she closed the gate making her way to the road in front, a strong feeling of being watched engulfed her. She was never wrong, and rather than look about, she went on her way, singularly fixed on her destination. Earlier, Gris had told her about going to Stoctun to enquire at the inn about what had happened at the farm and if anyone knew anything.

Brodin, Helga, Agatha, Magnus (who had changed his mind), and Badda queued at the church to go in for early morning service. Monks were outside the door selling wine, mead, and food. One very tall monk stood just inside the door with a collection bowl. It was in this congregation that Brodin and Helga soon realised that the residents did not bathe as frequently as they might. In fact, it was noticeable how less tidy the streets and houses were. The people whom Ebba introduced them to, however, were as nice as anyone could wish to meet. Christianity was certainly bringing out the best in people, they said to each other, not knowing that the pagans were equally friendly.

Gris had taken his small sword and dagger for defence in case of trouble, less noticeable when visiting an inn. He had taken a long walk into the town, leaving his horse to be fed and watered at the farm, ready for his and Myrte's separate journey. One thing he didn't have to worry about was his appearance making him stand out. People from all over the known world congregated in the town, with various styles of dress and hair. His first mission was to find a place to buy horses for Brodin and his family, having been given some money toward them.

The open woodland was eerie to those with superstitious fears. To Myrte, these were perfect conditions and surroundings to communicate with the spirits. As she moved in slow, furtive strides, there were many subtle noises, most of which were what she would expect, but there was a sudden crack. It was not of any animal nor any branch instantly falling to the ground. This was from someone who was quite heavily built and not too clever on his feet.

Myrte pretended not to be aware and started to prepare for her divination. She crouched, sat cross-legged in her heavy skirt, and then rolled back her sleeves, revealing various tattoos and a unique bangle.

Some thirty yards away, behind a dense bush, a tall, hefty figure stood watching the dark, mysterious sorceress, hypnotised by her every move.

Myrte soon determined where the man was as she summoned one of her guiding spirits. Slowly and silently, a pale green orb loomed toward her from the man's direction as if to indicate his presence. The orb grew larger and more elongated until it was the size of a man. Inside, it gave off flickering shapes, like bodies moving quickly past a window.

The man, whoever he was, did not linger any longer, running as fast as he could. Myrte concentrated on the figure looming forward in the vivid green corridor, not noticing the man had left. A full form never presented itself, merely an outline, and a resonance-like voice. All that mattered was that Myrte could hear in her mind what the spirit was saying. Her meeting went on for some time as she sat with her eyes rolled back, in some hypnotic state, a vehicle for the machinations of another world.

Gradually the corridor closed, and the wood that had gone completely silent started returning to normal life, a life with gusto. Birds were tweeting and singing, wild boar and a variety of other creatures rustling in the leaves and grass. Myrte slowly rose to her feet, dusted herself off, and grasped the charm on her wrist, saying, "Thank you for the power you have given me, and thank you for your wisdom."

Helga and Ebba were getting quite close by now, deep in conversation, as they all left the church. Brodin was starting to worry that his dreams may not be fulfilled. He interrupted their conversation by proposing they should all try to learn Latin to understand more of the Christian teachings. Helga was not too impressed with his interruption and gave a scornful look telling him that it would be unlikely they would ever have the time or the ability to learn,

"And who would teach us?" she chided.

Ebba smiled sympathetically at Brodin.

Magnus, meanwhile, was trailing behind, people-watching, being ushered along by his cousin, telling him he'd soon get lost in the crowd.

Badda was well-known in the town for being a bit of a gambler, and he didn't want Magnus to meet any of his less trustworthy associates. Unfortunately, that is exactly what happened, as coming out of a crowd of people, loomed one of the least savoury of his associates, who was also a murder suspect.

"Fair tidings Wagga," he said to Badda. Magnus looked on, confused. "Who's the little scraggins... do you want to put him up for wager?" asked the lout.

"Be lost, Feist!" said Badda, "Afore I bust your skull!"

Brodin looked back to see Magnus looking rather worried, standing in the middle of the busy street, Badda being hidden from view. He scurried toward Magnus and caught a glimpse of the minor skirmish Badda was having with Feist.

"I don't know what your business is, young man, but this is a holy day; we'll have no trouble here. Be on your way!" Brodin said to Feist in a very fiery temper. The scoundrel left, as he was told, seeing too much attention might be brought his way. Brodin did not lose his temper very often, but when he did, everyone knew about it.

CHAPTER NINE

The Horse Traders

Gris had sourced a pair of horses for sale, having asked the innkeeper during his midday meal and was told not to pay the price the traders would ask.

"They are greedy men," said the Innkeeper. "I would not go alone if I were you, they're not best trusted by anyone round here, but they're the only folk for miles with half-decent horses!" he added.

Not taking anything for granted, Gris decided to ask his sister to come along with him. He didn't have to look far for his sister, as he travelled back on the road which led him to town. She stood at the top of a rise in the road along with their horses, expecting him. Her bow was strapped across her chest and she was armed with her sabre.

"We have little choice today, brother. I have foreseen events in which we are about to partake. Utmost care is needed by us both. You know where we must go?" she asked.

"I do, sister, and I have already been warned of these men," replied Gris.

The road actually took them right past Edwin's farm, as the address of the trader was only half a mile off the mark. Everything was starting to fall into place, as Myrte had foreseen. Grey clouds suddenly billowed across the afternoon sky, followed by strong gusts of wind and fleeting bouts of hail storms. Gris opened the gate of the farm to allow their horses in.

They walked with their horses alongside towards the farmhouse. One of the farmhands who was hauling wood in the field called his master, who was behind the barn. As soon as he saw Myrte, he staggered slightly and gulped.

She knew instantly this was the man who had been watching her in the woods. He was a big, heavy man with a mass of hair. He was normally quite a rude brute, but his superstitious nature dictated his actions. The problem was his older brother quickly appeared out of the house, very similar in looks but somewhat brusque and down to earth. He came forward to ask Gris and Myrte what they wanted.

Gris said, "I understand you have some horses for sale. Would you happen to have a pair of cobs for a fair price?

The man replied, his eyes lighting up, "Aye, were you wanting to trade those steeds?"

"No-no-no, we are here to buy cobs or carthorses for our wagons. Two or three, depending on the price," answered Gris.

"Right, well, you'd best follow me. I have seven good cobs in this field," the man said, pointing beyond the barn.

True to his word, they were fine specimens. "I'll sell a pair for four geld and five pieces."

"How would three geld sound?" asked Gris, holding his well-stocked purse. Myrte had spotted two tall, ugly-looking men coming close, looking very suspicious. The other younger brother was looking on from a distance with a slightly worried appearance. Three more men suddenly came out of the barn.

"I think you could afford my price and maybe a little bit more," said the man menacingly.

Myrte said very calmly, "We'll split the difference and go on our way peaceably."

"I've heard a piece about you, lady. Your tricks won't work with me. That purse you carry is getting too much for you, my man... I think you ought to hand it to me," the man said, holding his hand out to Gris and nodding to his men to come closer.

No sooner had the man put out his hand, it was swiftly severed, cleanly and completely, from his wrist as Myrte lowered her bloody sword like a lightning bolt. The man screamed in agony as his two henchmen stood, not knowing what to do, and stared at the severed hand on the floor.

Myrte turned and waved her sword in readiness for battle as Gris drew out his sword. One of the men from the barn threw a pitchfork at Myrte, which she ducked and parried it away with her sword. The two other men had staffs, which they fancied to use against the brother and sister. Myrte ran speedily toward the men, quickly slashing their staffs to pieces, kicking one in the groin, and knocking the other one out with the hilt of her sabre. Gris stood in readiness as the other two looked on in shock.

The man who threw the pitchfork went to the aid of his father, who had lost his hand.

The two men, who had come first, stayed put as Gris guarded their every move. It was obvious they were hired hands with no blood ties.

Myrte turned towards the wounded man's younger brother, who had no intentions of getting his own hands dirty, instead, shouting for the others to do something. While she had her back turned, the wounded man quickly grabbed a knife from his son's belt and ran to stab Myrte in the back. Her hearing and keen senses brought her swiftly about, whereupon she cleaved the man's head wide open. He dropped to the floor, blood gushing everywhere during the death throes. The three sons who came from the barn were incensed with rage. The younger brother had now changed his mind, seeing his sibling being cruelly slaughtered, quickly grabbing another pitchfork from the barn. With mouth frothing anger, he charged at Myrte, only for her to sidestep his lunge and slit his throat.

"NOW STOP!" shouted Myrte. "Have you not learned your lesson?"

The first two men ran away towards the town, and the remaining brothers came to terms with the idea that they were bettered by skilled and dangerous fighting people.

Gris was always happy when he hadn't got to fight. Not that he wanted his sister to take over, just that she usually did, and he would fight if he had to.

The one brother that was still able declared that Gris and Myrte would not go unpunished. She walked up to him slowly and said, "We came here to buy horses. Your father tried to rob us and worse. You need to know what is right and what is wrong here. If you wish to live, you will declare what has happened in true account to the law. I can assure you, if you do not, I will have no hesitation in dispatching you as I have your father and uncle. And that goes for you also!" she said, pointing her sword at the other brothers still recovering from their assault.

It wasn't long before the Reeve came with several henchmen to the farm. The first part of the story was told by the two men who ran away. Fearing for their jobs, they said that Myrte and Gris suddenly became violent and that Gris had chopped off their Master's hand. They gave the credit to Gris, not wanting to appear being beaten by a woman.

The Reeve went straight to Gris and said, "Where were you standing when this happened?"

Gris told in full detail what had happened. The Reeve asked for his sword. Gris showed him, and the Reeve said, "No blood... now that's strange."

"He wiped it!" said one of the workers.

"On what and where?" asked the Reeve.

"Well, err-r-r..." spluttered the serf.

"And you, young lady, what has your part in all this really been?"

"She's a witch, and no two ways about it!" said one of the sons, still nursing his head.

Myrte looked into the Reeve's eyes and saw an honest, fair, and genuine man. He also noticed in her someone with a strong sense of justice, though not of his liking. She told it how it was. The Reeve listened intently while looking at the place, events, and bodies exactly as they lay.

"Did it not occur to you to get away and have no dealings with this family?" he asked.

"That prospect was not possible as this wretched man and his brother summoned everyone to surround us so they could take our money," answered Myrte.

The Reeve said to the remaining family and servants, "I have known of your misdeeds and damnable reputation in the town and its surroundings, but, until now, all have been without solid evidence. Here, you have more than met your match, and I shall forthwith be watching you all ever closer. I suggest you bury your father and uncle, give the horses to these people as part of your punishment, and... I strongly urge you to go about your business in an honest and respectable manner in the future."

Gris refused to take the horses for nothing, but the Reeve insisted they should have them and told them quietly to leave the area as soon as possible.

That evening, Gris told the family everything that had happened. Brodin was worried that his world was going to collapse with these *two crazy people* by his side.

"They are just going to invite trouble," he whispered to Helga later, who reluctantly agreed. Grimbald, Magnus, and Lars were in awe of Gris and Myrte, not taking on board the possibility of danger ahead.

Brodin decided they had better leave that night and had everyone packing.

Lars was up to his usual tricks of hiding things just as Brodin and his mother were putting them out.

"Edwin, I really would have you come too. I shall worry for your safety," said Helga.

"I know, mother, but I want to take my chances here. There are so many things to learn, and I get on well with my cousins. Also, chances are... that family won't be bothering anyone again. I think the Reeve sounds like he'll watch over everyone, alright," replied Edwin.

Myrte offered, "I sense your unease; we will accompany you part of the way. Do you know where you're heading?"

It was obvious Brodin was none too pleased about Gris and her riding with them, particularly as he felt like he was going off with three stolen horses.

"We are heading for Rheged, across the hills and moors, the other side of the country. Eadberht has told us of another cousin I had forgotten about, who has more than enough land and could probably help us get started again. We will probably have enough money to buy some land from him, I would hope."

Myrte and Gris did as they said; they packed their things and accompanied Brodin and family to the edges of the immense forest that went from north to south, as far as the eye could see. A shudder suddenly went up Grimbald's back at the same time as Myrte. They looked straightway at one another, she knew why, and he was going to find out.

Gris and Myrte said their goodbyes, and Myrte warned them to always be on their guard. "You really ought to teach the boys to fight," she said to Brodin.

"I am just a simple farmer who can wield an axe or staff, that's it!" he replied, half laughing.

"Make your way somewhat into the forest where you will find the western route but stay on to the main track and be on your guard at night," Myrte warned.

Brother and sister waved the family on and smiled. Agatha and the boys were all sad.

The last they'd ever see of each other in this world, Grimbald thought.

CHAPTER TEN

New Pastures

The family had been on the road for almost a week with a few worrying moments, one of which was caused by, guess who…?

Coming out of yet another part of the forest, they met a beautiful vista of magnificent hills and trees, far greener and more colourful than those back home. Everyone stood staring at the view and the surrounding farmsteads with a shimmering brook deep in the valley. The sun was half-risen but blindingly bright on the lush landscape. There was a wider road ahead, and Brodin decided they should follow it a little further north until reaching the next town or village before asking their way.

By late morning, the family hit upon a large hamlet. Brodin sent Grimbald and Magnus ahead to ask where they were and how far it was to 'Ulles wasser' where his cousin was believed to live. Magnus came back to tell his father while Grimbald lingered, curious about this odd place that followed some of the Roman lanes and paths, quite sprawling but not heavily populated.

"This is Saxby!" declared Magnus. "I think the man we spoke to said it was a full day's ride to 'Ulles wasser'," he added.

"And where is your brother," asked Brodin impatiently.

"Oh, he's hitherto?" said Magnus hopefully.

"I'll bet he's talking to girls," said Lar's, trying to cause trouble and teasing the geese with a stick.

"Leave them be, you devil," chided Helga.

Grimbald suddenly appeared from behind a large grain store.

"Well, Grim?" asked his father.

"Yes, where have you been?" added Lars cheekily.

Brodin cracked part of the reins on Lars' left ear while he was sneering at his brother. "And that'll be enough from you," said Brodin.

Lars called out in real pain, startled by his father's harshness; Helga stared angrily at her husband for such punishment. Grimbald told how he met an old man who told him exactly which was the best route to travel and which village would be best to ask for your cousin because they have a lot of markets there. And to keep going a few miles until they reach Apfelby.

It was late evening when the family managed to arrive at Apfelby. There was ample space to camp, with a wide flowing river, on what appeared to be free land, just on the outskirts of the village.

As they were starting to have supper, Lars called out, "Someone is coming, father. A fat man and two skinny ones!"

Helga told him to shut up before he got them all into trouble. It seemed the men never heard exactly what Lars said, but they were quite regimental in their attitude. They were local Huscarls.

 The fat one, as Lars described, ordered, "This is Lord Trewellyn's land, and if you want to stay here, you must pay a tariff. For one night, it is one and a half penningas. That means you can graze and water all your animals as well as yourselves but be of care that no one shits in our river, or you will have to pay a hefty fine, or worse."

Brodin paid the man from his purse and thanked 'his Lordship' for the privilege.

Lars walked behind the men at a distance imitating the fat man's plodding gate as Magnus called out to him loudly to come back, which caused the man to turn around. The man glowered and looked at Lars with fury, but he decided that it was late and he'd put up with his nonsense this time. Lars slinked back realising his stupidity, and started to remember the Thuringian soldiers again.

Magnus said to Grimbald, "Our brother is dangerous; he acts like we're still at home. No one knows him the way we do, and he could easily get us all into trouble."

"I know," said Grimbald, adding, "Father and mother really leave it too late sometimes to check him!"

"I heard that," said Lars defiantly.

"No bickering... be away to your beds," said Brodin, hearing the raised voices from the other side of the wagon as he urinated.

The pigs were a little unsettled, and the boar was becoming decidedly aggressive at one point, trying to escape his temporary pen. It soon became apparent why, as another family of travellers with a group of hunting hounds was settling down nearby. Then was the turn of the geese. Soon the noise was enough to wake the nearby residents, and people came out of their houses to see what the fuss was; most were annoyed by the disturbance. It wasn't too long before the Huscarls returned and, without question, moved the other travellers.

"Who were they, sir?" Grimbald walked over and asked the rotund leader.

"Gypsies, trying to sell their mangey hounds to those about, boy. We'll not be 'avin likes o' them round here!" the soldier said. "Nothing to fear," he added.

The night did not improve much as they were squeezed into the wagon altogether once more due to heavy rains. Lars did not sleep and just kept laughing and farting to order. The pigs and geese stayed unsettled also after the worry with the hounds. The full moon was playing its part too.

The next morning, quite early, there were many people milling about, local traders and farmers at their work. The field they were on was very boggy, and it would take some time to manoeuvre across to the main road. The new horses they'd acquired were obviously unused to these conditions and started to panic a little. Brodin realised shortly into their journey these horses would need a fair bit of training. This was simply fine for the tethered pigs as they were in their element. So, Grimbald walked the stock wagon up to the road, with the geese and pigs brought up behind by Magnus and Lars.

Brodin said to Helga, "You know, it's times like these, I wish Edwin were here. He'd have held the lads in check better and always a good man in troubled times." Just as the words had left his mouth, Lars started getting impatient with the geese and had them running in all directions by waving his stick at them viciously.

"LARS… YOU BLETHERING IDIOT IMP!" shouted Brodin as he launched himself off the wagon. Suddenly he was rolling on the ground in agony after twisting his ankle on a stone hidden beneath the boggy terrain. This event startled the horse, and it bolted off with Helga still in the back. Agatha started to cry, seeing her father in such pain and her mother carried off by the frightened horse.

Grimbald managed to recover the horse and wagon with the help of a local resident. His mother was dazed from knocking her head on the ground after falling from the wagon.

Helga had never really chastised Lars before, but this experience had brought home how irresponsible her son could be. She took the horsewhip from the front of the wagon and lashed Lars hard. As he turned his back to run, she hit his legs, flooring him where he stood. Lars' face hit the ground with a smack, and suddenly his whole front was covered in mud.

If it wasn't for the seriousness of his actions, his brothers would have burst out laughing. Some local bystanders did.

Now they had a problem. Father had either broken his ankle or sprained it badly, at the very least, and no one knew where the local healer was. She had been called away a couple of nights previously, and no one had seen her since. Helga knew how to make Brodin comfortable, but this was certainly not going to heal overnight.

One of the villagers saw what had happened and she told them that there was another healer in the direction they were travelling, who some people avoided, some say a demon in disguise, she did not know herself but said, "You will not have to look for him, he will pick you out and tend you."

Helga shuddered.

Eventually, the family was back on the open road passing a few other carts, wagons, and pedestrians in the damp and cloudy morning. The scent of fresh beet was in the air, prompting Brodin to consider buying fresh produce for the pigs. *They didn't seem to be keeping too well,* he thought.

It was approaching midday when the heavens opened. Lars just danced in the puddles and struck the long verge grass with his stick.

"Let him get his spirit together," said Helga as Grimbald attempted to grab him and pull him under the shelter of a large oak.

To the north of them was some open, stony ground beneath a long sloping hillside. As the rain eased, they could hear a gentle running stream almost hidden from view.

"A good place to water the animals again," said Brodin, wincing, as he lowered himself down tentatively from the wagon.

Grimbald, Magnus, Lars, and Agatha went ahead with the animals. Helga set about sorting some clothes to wash in the hope there would be enough dry weather to hang them on the wagon. Brodin hobbled along to the back of the wagon, checking on the wheels. Out of the blue, he saw the bottom half of a mustard-yellow robe. He straightened up to see in full view the figure, very tall and broad-shouldered with a heavy hood over his face. Despite the appearance, an overwhelming calm came upon him.

"Sit on that fallen log!" the stranger ordered in an awfully slow and strange Irish accent.

"What, here?" said Brodin.

"Yes, and remove your sock; it is wrapped far too tight. Now relax and let me feel your ankle," said the man. He removed his hood to reveal a man of about thirty years old, with blonde wavy hair, vivid yellow-green eyes, reddish-brown skin, and exceptionally clean looking.

"Ah yes, it is as I thought. You have a sprain; if you can take more pain, it will be cured in two days. If you want to take the natural course, I will say, two weeks at the very least."

"What will you do?" asked Brodin fearfully.

"Who are you talking to?" shouted Helga as she came to the rear of the wagon. "Oh my-y-y God," she added.

"Thank you for the compliment, my lady; therein is another ambition," joked the stranger with a wry smile. Then straightway grabbed Brodin's foot, twisted it inwards, chopping the outside with a hard blow and shoving a piece of cloth in his mouth before he screamed. Brodin passed out.

Helga shouted, "What on earth are you doing?"

The boys all turned their heads down the fields, out of sight, as Lars said, "Must be quarrelling again?"

The stranger continued, "If you do not know what I do, make it your duty to watch, you will learn something. (he noted her dower expression) Forgive me, lady; I am not a sociable man. I speak in facts rather than politeness. Many people complain about me. Your husband will be well in two days, and you can help; take these." He massaged and bandaged Brodin's foot afresh, then gave Helga a tisane and some ointment, instructing her how to use them.

Brodin was starting to come around. Helga knelt to comfort him, saying. "This man has given some medicaments to help you with your pain."

"What pain and what man?" said Brodin, woolly-headed, asking Helga to turn around and see the stranger gone as if swallowed up by the ground. She looked everywhere to find him but no sign.

"WE SHOULD PAY YOU, SIR," she shouted into thin air.

Brodin tutted and nodded his head. He cautiously rose to his feet, holding on to the log on which he sat. His ankle was tender and slightly weak, but there was amazingly no pain. *Whoever disfavours that stranger is an ass and a fool,* he thought, realising what had occurred.

Sometime later, the boys came back with the horses and the other animals. Their father was walking about almost normally.

Grimbald asked what he had done to repair his ankle.

"He was visited by an odd man... a healer," stated Helga, "I think he must have been the one the woman in the village mentioned?" She guessed.

"Ye gods father... you're well again!" said Lars following on.

"I am greatly improved, son... though I fear I will need to follow the advice given or else it may undo?" observed Brodin.

"Rightly so," added Helga, "and I think we should start with your tisane before we leave. Are all the animals watered and fed, boys?" she asked.

"Yes, mother, and tethered," replied Magnus.

"And has Lars managed to behave?" she enquired.

Magnus looked at Lars, then at Grimbald, and said, "Well, enough, mother."

Refreshed and all fed, they continued along the road to Ulles Wasser. Grimbald had found himself growing fonder of his family after all they had been through, but he was becoming a young man now, almost thirteen years old, and restlessness started to stir a strong need to know more about the world.

Another eight miles along the road, Brodin asked a man for directions to his cousin's place, Wynnstan of Lower Saxony in Modorby.

The small, middle-aged, ruddy-faced man smiled and said, laughing, "I am he... ha-hah-ha."

Everyone started to laugh except Lars. If he wasn't providing the merriment, he tended not to see the funny side of others. He just raised his eyebrows and announced, "I suppose we're here then?"

"You are indeed," said Wynnstan. "If here is where you want to be?" he added, still tittering to himself.

Brodin told Wynnstan about Cousin Edwin and his misfortunes and that his family said they would be able to make good in this part of the country. Wynnstan confirmed the possibility of them achieving what they wanted and offered to lead them to his farm and homestead, "All nice fresh food for supper!" he said, adding, "My wife is a wonderful cook; she would not let a man leave the table without a full belly!"

CHAPTER ELEVEN

The Settlement

It took nearly a month for the family to put their new farm to work, building new stockades and fencing, Wynnstan sending help occasionally. Even after purchasing the land from Wynnstan, Brodin had a reasonable sum of money left, enough to expand and hire some servants or buy/rescue some slaves. Being a relatively new Christian, the latter option was more in his mind to do. Helga was truly keen to observe the Christian ways and encouraged Brodin to try and free as many slaves as might be found.

"Be careful, my dear, we are merely Samaritans, not saints, and farming ones at that... and we do not yet know the way of things in this country; we must tread warily!" cautioned Brodin.

Lars overheard his parents talking and straight away said, "Can I have a slave mother?" To which she replied, "You already have one, my son... ME!"

Lars huffed, "I mean someone who does as I tell them."

Agatha, normally as quiet as a falling leaf, said, "I already do, brother!" and smiled shyly.

"Maybe your cousin Wynnstan could advise us?" suggested Helga.

"Aye, maybe?" Brodin replied. "We shall ask him tomorrow!" he added.

Brodin, as usual, saving his conversation for supper, told the whole family his plans and asked if anyone had any suggestions except Lars, who he knew would say something silly.

"We have a temporary home which we will need help to renew, and we cannot afford to lose much time preparing for market or getting livestock ready for sale. So, I must go to see what the situation is for acquiring workers." He announced.

The following day Brodin took Grimbald to Pennryd, where there were all types of markets and things for sale. Magnus, Lars, and Agatha were all given the task of borrowing stones out of one of the fields in preparation for growing corn. Helga was busy trying to make new clothes from cloth given by Wynnstan's wife, Eadgyd.

Life was beginning to take shape now, and the weather was somewhat better than back in Saxony.

A couple of hours down the road, father and son reached a terribly busy little market town. There were many side streets with traders of a wide variety of goods and street vendors selling tools, second-hand weapons, and wooden goods, like tables, chairs, and stools.

Soon they reached the bustling centre, where it was difficult to see exactly what was going on. It was full of smells, mainly bad ones, with sewage running down the middle of the street.

There were cock fights, bear baiting, punishment cages, where people would throw rotted food or worse, at the criminals, wrestling matches and bards or storytellers, standing, reciting sagas and legends from all lands with a lot of poetry and bawdy tales. There was a sizeable fish market, but most of it was dried and created a strange woody salty smell.

Over in the north end of the square was the slave market, most of whom were Picts or young people from poor families from all corners of Praedin (Britain). Sometimes the parents would actually be there to receive the ready money for the sale of their offspring.

Brodin found, from talking to one of the buyers, that some folk would just breed to make slaves and waste their lives on drink and gambling. "There's usually no work to be had from them sort; they're like their idle parents... no good for anything!" he said.

Grimbald suggested they watched what a particular man was doing as he had a very professional look about him. A woman standing next to Grimbald noticed what he was doing and said, "You'll not compete with the likes 'o him; he's the king's man. Buying for the king he is, he can pay what he likes, but the sellers usually let him have his serfs for the right price. Folk know not to bid against him."

Brodin said quietly, "This place disgusts me, my son, but we need help, and I will pay for two people as soon as I know what the right price is to pay."

They both watched what was happening, and after a length of time, some inner voice told Grimbald to use his instincts. "Feel the potential, not what you see now!" Looking very tired and bedraggled, just over halfway down the line, was a lean, angular-looking youth about Grimbald's age. He had a few bruises about his arms and face but a quietly determined look on his face. His wrists were sore from the manacles.

"Him, father", Grimbald whispered, grabbing his father's arm tightly.

"You think so?" enquired Brodin, rather puzzled. "Well, we had better see what price the lad will fetch?"

The auctioneer offered the boy at two pieces of silver. Most people laughed, thinking he was a troublesome belligerent young man who would be hard work for any owner. Slowly the price came down to seventeen pfennigs, and Brodin did the deed.

"GOOD LUCK with that one." Shouted the king's buyer, and everybody laughed.

Grimbald went to settle the cost with the auctioneer's second, then took the lad by the arm, but gently, and looked him in the eye saying as they grew further from the crowd. "We have not bought you... we have paid to have you as part of our household and family, or go free if you wish. If you work as we do, you will eat as we do. You will not sleep with the animals. You will live and sleep in our home."

The boy pulled his arm away, unsure what to believe, and said with a strong Irish accent. "You would be taking me for a fool. I'll not be anyone's arselick."

Brodin told Grimbald to tie the boy to the wagon wheel for now and explained that they should not do anything different to anyone else for fear of trouble. The boy looked at Grimbald in a told-you-so manner and shrugged his shoulders.

They still had another slave to buy, and some of the best bargains were gone, so to speak. Grimbald sneakily went to the back of the line-up to see who their next likely rescue could be, but his instincts were not as well-tuned as before. He struggled to spot a suitable candidate.

As he snuck back into the crowd to join his father, a girl slave broke into a fearful scream, who had been reccently sold to a brutish man. As the man had been sexually harassing her, she fought back and kicked him between the legs, whereupon he dragged her down the street and kicked her about the head and stomach. Some people watched in horror; others just tittered as she was just another awkward slave. The man told her to get up and go to his wagon, but her injuries were so bad she just could not move.

"Anyone wants this one for a boar or goat?" shouted the man.

"Five pfennigs," shouted one person.

"Seven" shouted another.

"I'll swap my wife," said one scruffy old man to everyone's laughter.

"Table and chairs," another; laughter again.

After some humour and some small arguments, Brodin stepped up and quietly offered the man fifteen pfennigs. The man saw someone in Brodin who could be easily handled and demanded a piece of silver. Brodin looked back at Grimbald for reassurance, who responded with a nod. The owner agreed his price with Brodin as he quickly pulled a piece of silver from his purse, rather reluctantly handing it to the man.

The man threw the girl at Brodin's feet, saying, "Me thinks you'll be sorry, old man, gingers are spawned with bad luck anyway!" referring to her bright red curly locks. The girl was still in a lot of pain, so Grimbald went to help her to her feet. Her face and hair were rather dirty, but as Grimbald looked upon her, he could see she was an attractive girl with more freckles than he had ever seen in his life.

Some other items on Brodin's list to buy were definitely going to be put on hold, but he felt a great sense of relief at what he had done. They bought some more feed for the animals and farm tools, but Brodin was slightly concerned at not being able to afford some weapons after being warned about raiders on the prowl in the area.

As the four journeyed on the road home a short way, Brodin suddenly stopped. He'd tied the two new recruits to the back of the wagon like everybody did, forcing them to walk behind. Grimbald protested at the outset, but Brodin knew it would be too risky to look so out of place.

"There were a lot of rough characters around, not so many Christian types around, I thought," observed Brodin and talking quietly so that the other two would not hear. "Now, the two of you, I will give you my trust by unfettering you both. You will sit upon the back of this wagon and know that we are to take you under our roof and treat you as free people," added Brodin.

He undid their manacles and gave them water to drink and wash themselves. They looked suspiciously at each other and the father and son who had taken them from the market. They rode quietly in the back of the wagon all the way to the farm. Trust was going to take time for the pair of them, but the alternative of running away was not an option, as most runaways were hunted down and beaten to death or left for the wolves to feast. Very few would go unscathed.

As the wagon arrived at the farm, Grimbald saw Lars at a distance waving a stick at a hooded man who just stood there laughing. As soon as the man saw the wagon, he disappeared over the wall and into nearby woodland.

The whole family came to greet Brodin and their new family members. The two slaves were overwhelmed by the friendliness of Brodin's family, and the girl started to smile, albeit warily and somewhat painfully.

Agatha went up first, face to face with the girl, and said, "Greetings, my name is Agatha; what are you called?"

The girl was hesitant and frowned slightly as if she'd forgotten, said, "I am Sunngifu, but everyone calls me Sunni."

Agatha was a little nervous, not knowing what to make of this profoundly serious guest.

Magnus and Lars introduced themselves to the boy, but when they asked his name, he declined and turned his back to look at the fields and countryside around him. Seeing this, Brodin realised the boy had possibly not seen such an open space in his life before. He instructed Grimbald to show the lad his sleeping space. It was only a corner of the temporary house allotted for the boys and Agatha, but it was cosy with ample skins and blankets for warmth. Agatha would now be allocated space with Sunni.

CHAPTER TWELVE

Family

There were a few trinkets and items the boys had collected over the years adorning the walls and table. It was going to be Grimbald's and whoever's task, to build new beds for everyone and partition the rest of the house to contain the animals etc.

The new boy was surprised at his treatment; he still couldn't believe people could be so kind and nice to him.

Lars didn't like the fact that the boy wouldn't talk to him properly and started aping the new boy's actions. One day the boy spun around, knowing full well what Lars was up to, and glared, saying, "Fyonn... and don't be fooling with me, boy!"

Helga caught what was going on and said, "Quite right, Fyonn. It's time you showed some respect, Lars. Clip the lad if you want Fyonn; he probably deserves it..."

"Mother, what are you saying?" interrupted Agatha, who was not quite sure about the newcomer.

"Thank you, lady," said Fyonn cautiously to Helga, then went about his new chores.

By midweek, Sunni was limping around trying to help with feeding the animals but fell to the floor with a thud, fainting from the pain. Helga was there in pen and quickly responded, calling for Magnus, who was nearby, and helped the girl to her bed.

"She is so white," said Magnus.

"Aye, and she needs more than we can give her, I fear. Go and see if your father can take her to Wynnstan's place and get some help. He will know," said Helga.

Magnus ran to his father and told him what had happened to Sunni. "I'll have a word with your mother, but we could do with getting this wall finished; the weather does not look favourable," stated Brodin.

Brodin entered the sleeping place and said to Helga, "Poor girl. God has not favoured her well. We will do as you suggest but could you take her... you and Magnus. Agatha is old enough to make a little supper. We will manage; just take the wagon... rest her in the back. I'll help put her in, make her comfortable, and see what can be done?"

Helga and Magnus rode off toward Wynnstan's farm, nearly seven miles south. The sun began to break through the clouds, and the gentle wind became a little warmer as the wagon rocked its way along the road.

Just under half the journey had been covered when the gentle breeze disappeared. The air became eerily still as the wagon approached a clump of trees and bushes. Their horse decided to pull up to a cautious stop, and suddenly, a tall figure appeared from a small side road.

Those yellow-green eyes and the ochre robe; symbols of the man's mystery. He looked at the mother and son, so matter of fact, and said in his own odd dialect, without being able to visibly see their passenger, "Let me look at the girl. I wager she will have to be left with me."

Magnus looked at his mother, then back at the stranger, mouth wide open.

The man went to the rear of the wagon and asked Sunni to try and lay out flat, which she did as if she could not disobey, had she even wanted to. The man then passed his right hand over her body closely without touching. "It is so! You will have to leave her with me. I am yet unsure how long she may take to heal," he instructed Helga.

Magnus and Helga had been almost unable to speak, and even when Magnus was about to interrupt, Helga held him back. She asked, "How will we know when she is well enough? And I did not pay you for your services to my husband."

The man answered cryptically, "Your payment is not necessary. I shall be rewarded sufficiently in time. You will know she is well when she will return," he then walked behind the bushes and brought out a donkey with a stretcher that had wheels attached to its base, and he smiled at Sunni saying, "Take this draft it will help with the pain!" He then helped Sunni very carefully onto the stretcher with sumptuous cushions to make her comfortable on the short journey. He whispered in the ear of the donkey and, without looking back, proceeded on his way.

Helga and Magnus made their way to the farm, speaking of their confusion to each other on the way. The man had beguiled them, yet they felt they had a strong sense of trust in him. As Sunni lay on the stretcher looking up at the cloudy sky, she felt a peace she had never experienced. Out of the corner of her eye, she could see the healer walking in front of the donkey. The animal was walking at an easy slow pace like it was magnetised to him without any tether. The ambience and the draft she was given compelled her to sleep. The next thing she knew, she was lying in a lovely comfortable bed with soft woollen blankets, completely fresh clothes, and smelling of something like lilac and honey.

Mother and son had returned early due to their strange encounter. Brodin and the rest were all too busy to notice. Agatha was trying to prepare a full supper; she had always helped her mother but had lacked the confidence in trying to do a complete meal for everyone. Seeing her mother arrive early was such a relief.

Helga got busy and showed Agatha the step-by-step approach to preparing a simple meal, making her more hands-on. Agatha was pleased with herself as if she had done it all. Helga smiled at her daughter's self-congratulation and said, rather tongue in cheek, "Well done, daughter, you see, you can do it, even without my help."

It wasn't long before Brodin and the others came in from the field. Fyonn had been working hard but was keeping himself aloof. Brodin thought *he'd 'let the lad come round in his own time.'* He could see Fyonn was able to appreciate his position but was still slightly suspicious of his new place in the world. While Helga was serving the food, Brodin asked how she came home so early. She told what had happened, after which Fyonn said, "I know him... the man you speak of. He's from my side of the waters... strange, strange man.

He's a shaman. Mochannain, I think he's called. Comes from a magical island to the west of Innis Fail, I heard?"

"Has he been in these parts long?" asked Magnus.

"Aye, quite long, but he moves about a lot... in the area. Some say he travels on the winds in a silver chariot... like a swift... and some say he's a goblin or such. From what I understand, he is waiting for something or someone," replied Fyonn with a frown.

Suddenly there was a barrage of questions about the shaman and Innis Fail, but Brodin told everyone to be quiet and eat their supper.

Brodin and Helga looked at each other with that thankful look, so pleased to see their recruit was coming out of his shell a little.

Several days went by, and as Brodin and family were coming from the fields for midday vittles, they saw Sunni walking through the main gate. She looked and felt as if she were renewed. Her hair was gleaming golden orange and crisply curled, her skin so smooth and unblemished. She smiled at everyone as she closed the gate.

Walking off in the distance was the Mochannain, with his donkey.

Helga caught sight of Sunni from the cooking place and immediately dropped what she was doing to greet the girl, hugging her and smiling kindly at her.

The weather was warm and sunny, so they decided to eat their midday meal at the outside table and hear what Sunni had to say.

Helga scrambled some extra food together for Sunni then they all waited with bated breath as she spoke.

"Well, I am just woken today, this very morn, and have been in a very strange place. After all these days, I found myself abed but washed and changed into the clothes I have now. In my time with Mochanna, there was a land of dreams I could not have ever imagined. People I had never met, places I had never been, and magical machines of all kinds. It was a place of wonder and elation. I wondered if I were in the Christian heaven, which I had never believed in before. One person in a golden robe told me I had been brought there by mistake and should return from whence I came. I did not want to leave that place, but Mochanna's soft voice brought me back. I believe he is an angel; he has made me more than new!"

Grimbald asked, "Did you see anyone you once knew in this place?"

"I thought for a short time, some of my family were there... but I could not see them," she replied.

Helga said, "Maybe Mochannain is an angel; he appears like one?"

Brodin remarked, "I doubt that he is an angel but a very clever man all the same, with many skills and talents."

Lars interjected, "Yes... but I'd bet he would be no good at farming or building walls."

"I would very much like to meet this man," said Grimbald curiously.

"I don't doubt you will, Grimbald, but only when he deems it so," said Sunni.

CHAPTER THIRTEEN

Much to Pay for

So much happened during the family's migration, but things started to quieten down eventually. The farm grew more and more prosperous with a few minor hiccups. A proper longhouse was built to secure the animals; their presence would provide warmth for the family during winter.

Brodin had managed to buy two more slaves and offered their freedom at his home.

Everyone got on very well most of the time, but Lars seemed to be becoming more precocious. He liked to tell fibs about people and cause arguments, but he was not so funny anymore, being more of an annoyance. Nearly every one began to question where his stories came from and quickly verified his mischief. It soon came about that hardly anyone took any notice of him anymore, so his restless spirit began troubling their neighbours. Sometimes he would tie their geese's heads together or cover them in swill or both. Occasionally he'd just terrify the animals. Then he would have his little chuckle when the neighbours would call to question if the family had seen anything going on.

Unluckily for him, one day, he had a rider fall off his horse after jumping out to startle him. The man happened to be one of the Reeve of Penrydd's Huscarls. Lars was taken to Penrydd for a public flogging.

The shame on Brodin's family was a heavy burden for him, who argued with Helga about sending Lars elsewhere. They both always agreed how unlike Lars and Agatha were, considering they were twins. "Perhaps the devil himself had his part in his coming," remarked Brodin.

Even Wynnstan and his family would keep their distance after the public embarrassment. Apart from all that, the Reeve had given orders to his men not to attend Brodin's family as being a part of his protectorate. Not that the family had ever noticed anyone looking out for them.

Helga no longer tolerated any of Lars' misdeeds and would duly punish him with less food and extra chores. Through all this, he persisted, "As if possessed by the god Loki," said Grimbald.

Fyonn could not stand to be around Lars and avoided him at all costs. By the second summer, Fyonn had embraced his newfound freedom and would work harder than he had ever done for Brodin and his family. He showed skills that

Brodin and the boys did not have, like the caring and maintenance of the horses and the new mule. He had a way with all the animals and was a great asset.

Sunni also worked extremely hard. Consequently, Helga became more of a lady of leisure, particularly with the other new servant assisting Sunni.

The man-servant assigned to Fyonn was not a very fit one, having been employed in the lead mines. Though he tried his best, all the while, Fyonn was very patient. The new man had a certain charisma, and it soon became a very positive element in the family circle.

Brodin had, at last, and in a truly short space of time, achieved most of what he set out to do, and life was on track. But Brodin being who he was, never took anything for granted. The security of his home and livelihood were at the forefront of his mind. All his family loved him and would do their utmost to assist him, as they all promised after an evening's discussion around the supper table. Even Lars tried to show some concern.

The new man, Brynn, was the only one now who took any interest in Lars and felt rather sorry for him. They would often play games that were common practice for Brynn but unheard of by the family. It turned out that Brynn was quite an asset in taming the wild young redhead. Lars would constantly ask Brynn questions about where he grew up and what people did. The Wahller was very fanciful with his tales and often used to sing of legendary giants, Faerie folk, and the like. Though most of the family took him with a pinch of salt, Magnus, Agatha, and Lars were enrapt. With Brynn, Fyonn, and Sunni around the family was never short of entertainment.

Sunni, in her own right, had a way of telling things that often came out in a humorous fashion or simply made silly mistakes that made people laugh. She was very good-natured and knew her own faults all too well.

Lars eventually did his best to win over extended family and neighbours. He barely ever lapsed into his old ways. Sadly, not everyone was so trusting of his turning over a new leaf.

Eventually, Brodin and Helga had managed to persuade Fyonn, Sunni, and Iphina, the new girl, to attend church on Sonnandaeg, though Fyonn really went along to please his master.

There was still some hesitation on the part of Wynnstan and his family even though they knew they should forgive; like many people in their time, pride got in the way.

As an extra penance, Brodin made Lars do double chores for his neighbours, which helped greatly in restoring some of the family's standing in the community. And Lars realised how much trouble he had been for once!

CHAPTER FOURTEEN

The Silence

Toward the third autumn, after harvesting his first field of corn in Rheged, Brodin got sick. Helga was worried about what would happen if she were left to make good on her own. Of course, Grimbald was a hard-working young man who could take on most of his father's responsibilities, but things were still not great with Wynnstan and their neighbours since Lars' trouble. The family was not really able to seek assistance elsewhere, so they had to work very hard, and Magnus pulled out all his reserves to aid his elder brother.

Fyonn had more than proved himself and was a constant source of entertainment with his stories and superstitions. In what little time he had to spare, he had been making a special chair for Brodin and was now worried that it would not be finished in time.

Helga racked her brains for a remedy, but it was Sunni who came up with a broth that might help. She suddenly gave a list of ingredients that she and Helga must gather. "I know not whence that came?" she declared. They later picked wild nettle, garlic, and sorrel. "All this, goose's liver chopped, fried in the goose's fat, and boiled in a pail of water with a half cup of brown salt," announced Sunni. Everyone in the family was given a little, and they thoroughly enjoyed it.

Brodin was given the broth first, and whether it was that which brought about his recovery or not, no one could be sure. Perhaps the fresh ale and bread had helped. However, he made a full recovery. The only mystery was why the illness had struck just him. He didn't want to think about the question as he was eager to return to work.

Grimbald had really feared the worst, and a great sense of foreboding came over him. Everyone else, however, seemed to have confidence that father would pull through.

It was on Lordag, the day before church when Lars was down-field catching a stray goose totally fixed on his quarry. The sound and sight of horses' hooves trotting towards him caught his attention. There were three men, all looking very sinister. The man at the front had a huge belly and skinny legs, with long thinning hair, and a large bald patch. Lars wanted to hold his nose, as they all smelled terrible. The leader asked Lars in a creepy kind of way if he knew where they might get some fresh water in his thick Irish accent.

Lars was now more aware of his limitations and said politely they could have water from the farm's well! "This way!" he said, pointing south toward the farmyard. Suddenly one of the men flew off his horse in Lars' direction, then just as suddenly skirted off to one side saying something in Gaelic, and quickly caught the stray goose by the neck, its wings flapping for dear life, and handing it straight back to Lars without hardly looking at him.

The three men rode ahead of Lars toward the farm and out of sight into the yard about a quarter of a mile away. When Lars got back to the yard, his father was just finishing talking to the leader. One of the riders, a scruffy man with a mop of black hair, looked over his shoulder at Lars with a sinister smile. This man really did not like him.

The next morning, Brodin, Helga, and Agatha made their way to church along the road to Penrydd when they saw a group of men lingering suspiciously in nearby woodland. Whatever they were doing, they seemed not to notice Brodin and his family, much to Brodin's relief.

On their way into the church, Brodin almost bumped into Wynnstan and his family in the busy throng at the church door. Wynnstan decided it would be better to build bridges again with his cousin's family. They spoke quite formally at first and agreed to carry on their conversation after the service.

The huge wooden church was full to the walls and became very warm by the latter part of the service. Even the Reeve and his Huscarls at the front of the church were sweating profusely. Agatha asked her mother if she could go outside as she felt she would faint. Helga told her to be discreet, to put her shawl over her head, and slip out of the side door as quietly as possible. Agatha managed to scuffle through with some difficulty receiving some disdaining looks on the way. She opened and shut the door very quickly and took a deep gulp of fresh air.

The church stood on a high mound that replaced an ancient barrow looking over the town. There were a few gravestones belonging to esteemed nobility with a scattering of young yew trees and wild gorse. Some locals were allowed to graze their sheep and goats to help keep the grass down.

Agatha was looking down to the main road, which was noticeably quiet. Feeling somewhat refreshed, she listened carefully at the door to hear if the service was nearly over. There was a soft fine rain coming down on a gentle breeze when she momentarily heard the clip-clop of horses' hooves. As she looked down to the front of the church, a troupe of shabby figures appeared from around the church gate, led unmistakably by the same man that had come into the farmyard the previous day. They travelled up the main street, as the leader casually looked around, spying on Agatha who tried to slink back behind a church buttress, out of site. He stared at her; a sickly-sweet smile crept over his face. She cringed with horror but tried not to show it. Some of the other men looked as well, making her feel terribly nauseous. She felt even worse and more afraid than she felt before.

Not long after the event, the service ended, and everyone started ambling out once the Reeve and Abbot had decided they could. Brodin saw Agatha slinking away at the side of the church, trying not to be noticed for the sake of disapproval.

"You look not too well, my girl. Shall we take you home forthwith?" asked Brodin.

"Could you, please, father," she whispered.

Just before they mounted the wagon to go home, Wynnstan called to Brodin, "Brodin, I have something to tell thee!"

Helga and Agatha stood beside the wagon out of earshot as Brodin spoke to Wynnstan. They stood for some time, and Wynnstan said loudly at the end. "Promise me you will, cousin."

Both families waved to each other as they took a separate fork in the road. Helga asked Brodin about Wynnstan, but before he could reply, Agatha reported, "I saw that horrible man again with many more men following him… he made me feel sick again when he looked at me and smiled. I think he's really bad?"

"The one that called in the farmyard yesterday do you mean?" asked Helga.

"M-m-m yes, mother, him," she answered.

"This may be of what Wynnstan talks?" said Brodin.

Back at the farm, the boys and men servants had been busy working, building new pens for their newly acquired sheep, while the girls were up early milking and feeding the cattle. Sunni told the new girl, Iphina, "I'll boil some water for us to bathe whilst there be peace and quiet."

It was a warm autumn day, and the girls had gone through a tough time with some of the cattle, so they went to the storehouse for a strip bath. Iphina didn't take long and was soon in the kitchen preparing the morning meal.

Meanwhile, Sunni decided to wash her hair in the remaining bowl of water. Just as she started to wring and dry her hair, Grimbald walked in. They had seen each other naked before, at a distance, when they went for a community bath at the lake. But this moment was exciting and awkward at the same time, for both.

Sunni was a few years older than Grimbald, though she thought, what a handsome young man he was growing into. Half pulling her robes toward her, she smiled at Grimbald warmly and put her arm around his neck. She helped undress him. There was a meeting of minds and bodies without complete innocence, for they were constant witnesses to the animals, the gruntings and groanings of Brodin and Helga, or just stumbling on many a couple, merrymaking in the fields.

The lovemaking was warm and relaxed; even after their bonding, they spoke for a short while, swapping pleasantries, then Grimbald suddenly realised what he had come to the store for.

"I'd better get the rasp and claw for the animal's hooves afore Lars comes to stir up trouble!"

Grimbald quickly dressed, and luckily enough Lars was coming to look for him, taking so long to find the tools. Grimbald was smiling away as if he was walking on air. He had opened the door to becoming a man; it was his first and most magnificent time.

"What are you smiling about?" asked Lars. "Are you possessed?"

"Nay, brother, just at peace with the world," replied Grimbald, juggling the tools as he walked.

"Aye, you're assuredly possessed!" said Lars.

Brodin, Helga, and Agatha arrived back a short while later. Eventually, they all sat around the huge dining table, which was placed conveniently close to a window where Brodin could look out onto his new, nearly finished longhouse. Grimbald and Sunni glanced furtively at each other.

"I have something to tell!" said Brodin. "Your uncle Wynnstan and I are back on talking terms. We spoke early this morning after Church. He has warned us of the presence of brigands from Ireland, possibly the very men we had met in the farmyard yesterday and whom little Agatha saw this morning riding through Penrydd. I will try to gain the support of the Reeve tomorrow in case we are the target of these loathsome creatures. You will come with me, Lars, to show how much you have repented your actions and plead our case."

Lars was uncommonly quiet and somewhat embarrassed, as was shown in the colour of his cheeks. He only liked a full audience when he was ringmaster, not quite so much now, but his silence was a satisfactory acknowledgement of his compliance.

Fyonn asked Brodin, if he knew where in Ireland the thieves might be from, thinking he might be able to intervene, and was disappointed with the answer that he could not help.

As befitted their holy day, Brodin and Helga insisted they do as little as possible. Yet there were disturbing sounds in the far distance, and some of the animals were behaving skittishly in the far fields. That Sunday evening was an unsettled one, and nobody slept well.

The following morning was a lovely, warm, scent-filled morning. Grimbald had gone fishing at the lake.

Brodin and Lars readied themselves for a meeting with the Reeve, just taking the horse and hen cart. Brodin reached down to pull the reins from the floor while Lars sat and watched him when three arrows shuddered into Brodin's neck, chest, and thigh. His screams were silenced by the arrow in his neck, blood pouring out of his wound.

A fourth arrow skimmed off the flesh on Lars' left shoulder; he, too, reeled in agony, squinting to see his father grasping desperately at the wheel of the cart. He screamed and cried with pain. Lars fell from the cart and automatically started to run… anywhere but away, sobbing as he went.

Brodin staggered around aimlessly, spluttering and gargling in his own blood before falling dead at Lars' feet.

The thundering of horses' hooves was deafening. Magnus tried to run but was just trampled down and killed instantly. Brynn, the ex-miner, attempted to fend three of the raiders off quite valiantly with his pitchfork, killing one and wounding two others before being beheaded by the leader's sword.

Helga and the girls were inside talking to Fyonn when the disturbance first broke out. Helga saw out of the window what had happened and told them all to run and save themselves, to see if they could find sanctuary with Wynnstan. Sunni insisted on staying.

Agatha was instructed to go with Fyonn, who would be able to save her. He, too, did not want to go. Helga was sobbing and pleaded with Fyonn as the only man left to do as she instructed. Eventually, he did as asked and plotted an escape route along the dykes and hedgerows. Iphina agreed to accompany him and Agatha. Fyonn planned to break his way through the cold store next to the nearby dyke, but he would have to hurry; the boards and wire were strong.

Helga went out with a spear, shaking and trembling, in order to buy Fyonn some time. Sunni came out a moment after, wielding an axe and short sword. She made the men laugh at first, being slimmer and smaller than Helga but soon proved to be a worthy opponent. Two men who were about to take her were both badly wounded, and as she turned to fight off a few that were turning on Helga, there was an almighty thud to the back of her head as one giant man wielded his club on her. Sunni fell like a stone to the ground. The leader ordered his giant accomplice to bring her with them.

Helga screamed at the men to leave them and take what they wanted. Agatha couldn't bear to hear mother's screams and dashed out to help her as Iphina tried to pull her back. Iphina was distraught and told Fyonn she was going to do what she could to help, but he reasoned that escape was the only option. "If you want to live, come with me. Our chances are better on the run," he insisted.

Agatha was clinging to her mother's arm when four of the ugly raiders seized them both without much of a fight.

"Please do not harm my daughter," pleaded Helga.

" Very well, bring the girl," ordered the leader.

"No – no – no…" Helga begged.

"What about this one?" asked one of the men, pointing to Helga.

"As you wish," he replied with a nod of his head.

Helga was dragged out of sight and brutally raped by several men while screaming out for Agatha.

"Shut her up," said one.

Another who was dressing himself turned quickly and cut Helga's throat while she was still being raped.

"Sheiss," said the other rapist in shock as her blood spurted in his face, showing nothing for his victim.

The giant one came around the corner and looked at them all in disgust without saying a word.

Helga's dress was left turned up to her waist, leaving her body exposed, as the men casually walked away, leaving her bloodied corpse with eyes wide open from the horror.

The giant returned, covered Helga's legs, and closed her eyes, immediately rushing off to join the other men.

"MOVE AND FAST," ordered the Chieftain. To which they did. "Wait, get that boy and string him up. I don't like that little insolent, freckled toad sperm."

Lars was trying to run through the field to a nearby wall, holding his shoulder tightly as the blood raced out of his wound. He thought he could hide when suddenly two men picked him up and dragged him between their horses back to the farmyard, his feet catching the rough ground as he went. He tried to show courage, but tears streamed down his face, even more so when he caught sight of his mother's body. There was no more fight left in him as the men put a rope around his neck. He just stared at the leader with contempt and in silence as his body was then thrown into the newly built well.

The men left with their hoard quicker than they arrived as voices on the horizon grew nearer.

CHAPTER FIFTEEN

The Enlightenment

Grimbald could hear loud voices and screaming as he returned from his fishing excursion, unaware that those screams would be the last he would ever hear of his family when he climbed the southern wall with his catch. He looked towards the western horizon, where he saw a group of riders with carts and wagons that looked like the ones on the farm. He also heard a young girl's scream that sounded very like Agatha, suddenly, he realised what must have happened as he could make out Sunni, strewn over one of the rider's horses, galloping off into the distance.

Memories of what Myrte had told him flashed through his mind. He wanted to scream out as tears rolled down his cheeks. He looked over the adjoining wall and saw his father's body lying in the yard; three arrows sticking out from him and a pool of blood that told Grimbald there would be no life left in him.

Before he took another step... all that had happened before his arrival scurried through his mind, every action, every scene, and every sound as if he were a fly, witnessing everything unnoticed. At this point, his emotions were overwhelming, and he fell unconscious where he stood. However, a soft glowing amber shape loomed towards him that seemed to float above the ground.

Seven miles down the road, an exhausted, frightened young man and girl arrived at Wynnstan's farm. As they opened the gate, one of Wynnstan's servants recognised Fyonn from a previous visit and ushered him and Iphina into the majestic longhouse.

Wynnstan had been disciplining one of his other servants for neglect of his duties when Fyonn interrupted him to tell of the terrible incident at his cousin's farm.

"Oh, my god, how bad is it? I feared it could happen, but never thought ..." said Wynnstan in shock.

"What on earth has happened, my dear?" asked his wife.

Fyonn explained more fully what he had witnessed, apologising for not being able to save Agatha, and said they would need the help of many men if anything could still be done.

"You must take some men now and see what you can do." Insisted Wynnstan's wife. "And I shall come also. I can still fight! I'll send word to the Reeve. Ulrich and Edwin must be informed. We must find the couriers," she added.

None of them would be prepared for the horrors they were about to meet.

Grimbald recovered consciousness but in a slow way. Waves of imagery flashed disturbingly before his eyes, seeing his father and mother holding hands and smiling reassuringly at him.

Gradually he became aware of his surroundings and surmised that he was in the home of the wizard Sunni spoke of. It was just a moderate, single, cup-shaped lodge of wattle and daub with a small hole in the middle to let out the smoke. The fire was directly in the middle, and Grimbald lay on a soft mattress beside it. As he looked around, still blurry-eyed, he saw a ferret standing upright, staring straight at him.

Suddenly, a soft Irish voice came from a few feet away, out of view, at the strange-looking entrance door, "Do not be afraid young man, that is Whip. He always looks over strangers, very suspicious he is. Give him time... he'll come around you."

Grimbald's mind started working overtime; he felt unsure and remembered stories of wizards having familiars, a magic spirit that was part of their host. Even through all that had happened, his fears grew stronger in this man's presence. He determined he would escape at his first opportunity.

"No, you will not. You're mine now!" said the man in a sinister tone.

Grimbald started to sit up. As he looked at the man, he noticed a friendly grin on his face, which turned into a loud guffaw.

"I know what you are about to ask, and yes, I did. I read your mind, young man. Do not worry; I cannot always do so. It happens much like clouds on a rainy day," said the wizard. "I think my mind has more clear sky in it today," he joked.

Grimbald looked at his host, very confused. He asked why he was there.

"We need each other young man. You need to learn, and I need to teach and learn… it was in the runes. So there's nothing to argue over, they're always right, and I must do their bidding. Besides, I have dwelt alone far too long," he stated.

"But I must attend to the funerary affairs of my family. I cannot leave their bodies for wild animals, and there is the matter of my sister and Sunni being kidnapped by those evil men. I must try to rescue them somehow," pleaded Grimbald.

The wizard had his back turned toward Grimbald at this point, putting things away on shelves. He had the manner of an extremely busy man but in a fairly quiet, calm way. "Everyone and everything has its optimum time, young man, and for now, you and I are going to move away from here." He turned around to speak face-to-face. "All that you care or worry about at this moment will be attended to by your friends and remaining family. Your life is to take on a new and particularly important course... as will mine. I am called Mochannain Mattoch of the Tuatha de Danaan, Mochanna to you," he snapped with a quick smile.

Grimbald still felt unsure about his circumstances, but curiosity and an underlying sense of trust were starting to form in his mind. He thought about what he had to go back to and how he would be able to get his sister and Sunni back. Perhaps it was better if they, his uncle and family, thought he was dead for now and to see if there really was something more for him, as Mochanna promised, maybe something that could help.

"We will travel at first light tomorrow," ordered Mochanna.

"Where are we going?" asked Grimbald.

"Should that matter, Grimbald?" said Mochanna as he sat cross-legged on his bed, playing with a stray wildcat kitten.

"Well, it's in the spirit of a man to wish to know his destination," replied Grimbald.

"And what is wrong with not knowing? The mystery, the magic of anticipation, is surely stronger for not knowing. Enjoy that," he replied. "Man has too many problems in trying to find certainty in his life and planning... all the time planning. Such waste!"

The following morning was not very bright, with a soft mist coming off the land. As Grimbald turned to sleep a little longer beside the less-than-warm embers of the fire, he felt a nudge in his back, quite heavy but soft. He thought something must have rolled against him. As he turned to look, he near jumped out of his skin as he came face to face with Mochanna's donkey. He coughed and spluttered, half choking while the beast just blew hot air onto his face, down its broad, deep nostrils.

Mochanna was turned to the wall, cosily curled under a soft blanket with his hood over his head. He woke a little with the sound of Grimbald's fright.

"Did you not say we were going on our travels this morn?" asked Grimbald.

"Well, how is the weather outside, my young man?" replied Mochanna, not stirring.

"I believe it is going to be kind," pondered Grimbald.

"Well, if that is so, we shall set sail forthwith," the man joked, pulling his hood onto his shoulders and sitting upright. "Should we have something to eat first, do you think?" he added.

"If we are to travel far, I would suggest we do, sir," said Grimbald.

"And what if we do not travel far, sir?" said Mochanna sarcastically, adding as he rose from his bed. "If I say to you, I do not know where or how far we are going. Do you say we eat heartily, as it may not be necessary and slow our journey, or do we eat meagrely, for it may not be enough to sustain us? And call me master, for that is what I shall be, should you wish it?"

Grimbald was totally unaccustomed to having to think in this way and pondered for some time. "We should eat moderately, master... for then we can rest if we need to gain our strength."

"M-m-m good," replied the man cryptically.

Myrte's words were suddenly looming in Grimbald's thoughts. This must be the man she spoke of, the sorcerer and scholar she so admired. The man she envied Grimbald for, having such a tutor.

Mochanna picked up a little of what Grimbald was thinking and stared curiously at him, trying to unravel a little more. It happened to be one of his less tuned-in moments.

"Are you reading my mind again?" asked Grimbald.

"None too well," the sorcerer replied. "Either I'm foggy, or you are," he added sarcastically.

"Might I ask master what I will learn from you, and am I bound to you in any way, for however long in my learning?" Grimbald enquired.

"You are not bound to me in any way, young man, but the fates determine you should remain with me for your tutelage for at least three years. I will teach you herbal medicine, the ways of Wyrd, the ways of a champion warrior, and how to be a good man. Enlightenment. How does that sound?" asked Mochanna with a wry look on his face.

Grimbald looked at him, very confused. "I don't know what to say... except I would not have thought of you teaching me the ways of a warrior?"

"There are many types of warriors of whom I am well versed, and you shall know the best of their ways from many different countries, for that is a part of your destiny. You will manage yourself in such a way that you will cause mystery among your fellow beings and, in turn, become a mystery to yourself. There shall be no pride in what you achieve against your enemies, only a cautious pride in what you make of yourself. Never be self-satisfied, for that is the root of arrogance and folly," stated Mochanna.

Grimbald was beginning to realise what Myrte had alluded to. This man was such a strange mixture of strong character, unassuming manner, enormous knowledge, and charming eccentricity. He simply couldn't help but like him.

Suddenly Mochanna stopped everything he was doing, pulled up his robe between his legs, tied it with the sash around his waist, and said, "Wait here." Then he ran off through the woods faster than any man Grimbald had ever seen, to where he did not know or for how long, and it was long...

Nine days went by, and Grimbald constantly debated with himself whether to go back to the remaining people he knew and take the animals there with him or just stay put. He did, after all, feel responsible for the creatures that Mochanna had rescued. His senses told him there was something imminent about to happen, but it didn't feel

128

good. Grimbald shared food with the wildcat, fed and watered the donkey, and during his time alone, noticed a pack of wolves in the vicinity that, for some reason, came close to his small camp but did not behave quite as expected. Another regular visitor to the camp was a crow who would not go away until offered some food, constantly staring with one eye at Grimbald and tilting his head back and forth as if he were trying to say something.

The boy went out of the hut, as usual, to scour the edge of the woods and the lands about him before it grew dark. Grimbald decided it was time to go in and make a fresh fire. Just as he got close to the hut, he heard a crackling sound. "I must be going mad, too long a time on my own; that sounds and smells like a fire to me. I do not remember lighting…" As he entered the hut, there sat naked in front of a large fire was Mochanna, trying to boil some water.

"Master, where have you been? Are you well?" asked Grimbald, quite worried, surprised, and noticing blood spatters on his master's muscular hands, arms, and legs.

"I am well enough, young Grimbald," replied Mochanna in his usual cryptic manner. "And how are you?" he added while washing his hands in the warming water. "You might press for me, a clean robe, from that trunk beneath my bed, if you, please? And I will tell you more."

Grimbald raked back some embers and placed the press on them to warm, saying, "I had doubts about your return master, and debated my circumstances here. Not exactly being the king's cook, I managed with hunting and foraging and made acceptable offerings for myself and these creatures here," he said, nodding his head in the direction of the hyperactive kitten. The donkey stood in the doorway, staring at the playful feline.

"I have the desire for a draft of mead; bring me that flask and a chalice," commanded Mochanna, casually pointing to a large teardrop-shaped pot as he washed his hands and arms.

Grimbald handed over the freshly pressed garment.

"Now I shall tell you all. For you must be made aware of the politics and machinations of those who take power or attempt to," said the wizard as he got dressed in his nicely pressed ochre robe.

He continued in a very matter-of-fact way, "Firstly, I did something I would rarely do... I intervened in the certain slaughter of a small group of people, which would have taken place without my presence. This was of no satisfaction to me... but for the extinction of some who were evil doers, I did take some sense of accomplishment. There is a war brewing in the near vicinity once again, and this time it is for a greater portion of these lands. Another pretender to a mythical lineage is greedily and cruelly seeking power over us all. I may not stop him, though I could, but the fates have decided he must follow his course and meet his destiny like many before and after. He will eventually succumb to the machinations of the new Roman beliefs and corruptions. I shall, however, become a nuisance to him albeit invisible, and therein you shall learn greater skills than that of a warrior. You must first learn to be a ghost. But we must move from this place today. Prepare the cart and food items for our friend Huffcare (the donkey) to bring."

Grimbald was sad to be moving further away from the connections to his past but realised a new life and destiny lay before him, yet still promising himself to find his dear young sister.

CHAPTER SIXTEEN

The Schooling

693 AD

The camp had moved on to another location, and Grimbald was starting to learn a number of small skills from his master, but most of all, he was learning to be patient and not to expect anything. Some of his lessons required fast learning and travelling, which was getting uncomfortable. He would constantly ask, "Where are we, master?" Nearly all the time, he met with silence.

However, one day Mochanna replied, "Does that really matter, young man we are here, and that is enough of a place name! Just be sure of your direction and where the sun is or hides."

Wars were raging everywhere now, not resulting in huge massacres but in constant raids and heavy assaults. East, west, north, and south; the country was full of pseudo-lords and kings. Christianity was bribing and bullying its way into Anglo-Saxon society. Many reeves and thanes were unsure whom to ally with. Those were uncertain times. However, one man wasn't, Mochannain Mattoch.

Rhoedd was an ambitious and fearsome king who had begun to rule most of northern, central, and western Britain. He was attempting to emulate his grandfather, Urien, whose influence on the way of life in that region would last for centuries to come in forming its own identity. The true Cwmbran identity would be forged in Ogledd Rheged and De Rheged.

Many Pictish and Irish descendants amalgamated with Rhoedd to keep the Cwmbran unity and character in their last great battle with the Saxons.

Mochanna now had to fast-track Grimbald's learning to aid in some small part in the outcome of the war and to further the young man's passage into adulthood.

One evening, Mochanna spoke for an exceptionally long time regarding the do's and don'ts of the Ways of Wyrd, explaining about the Norns being the guides of past, present, and future. He further related the tale of how Odin lost his eye in the quest for wisdom, but instead of all the elaborations that many shamans would use, he put all the main stories into a common-sense set of values. He did, however, advise Grimbald to move slowly along the edge of the spiritual world until he found sureness of pace and footing. "Remember the web," he would say rather cryptically. "It will tremble?"

"The spirits can also lie, young master, and many would have you flounder. Do not accept all they tell or reveal to you and call upon your ancestors or your spirit guides to help you. If you give them your faith and trust, they will help you in many ways that you may not imagine.

Look now around you. Everything that you see has the spirit of nature within it, whether it be the broken leg of a chair or the hair that has fallen from your head, even the bones that remain from our departed. They have the contract of nature, an existence in form without thought or animation. They are a part of the cradle of the elder Norn. What we see about nature is an imagining and mixture of the minds of many higher spirits. Like the Norns, we have a trinity of elements, the material, the spiritual, and thought, all three essential to each other and infinite. We must not perceive death as an end; it is merely a change, albeit seemingly quick at times.

Most of us move at a certain pace and think as if life should be equally measured for all creatures but look how fast the shrew darts through the leaves in the forest. To the shrew, we must look lumberingly slow, and what about the common fly who moves faster still? We must look as slow as the sunrise?"

Mochanna talked on about the meaning of life as Grimbald's eyes grew heavy until he just slumped into a heap across the straw-laden floor and fell into a deep sleep. Mochanna slowly moved over to the young apprentice and whispered in his ear for a short while before retiring to bed himself.

The next morning, Grimbald woke with a great rush of energy and clarity of mind. Mochanna was sitting by the fire, back turned, making a broth of wild oats and vegetables. For whatever reason, he always threw into the pot a sizeable stone from a nearby river.

Grimbald had not asked before, as so many of Mochanna's actions were strange and unfathomable, but an instant notion came over him. "The stone; it represents the earth and all that is about us, and food is necessary to every living thing. You make all meals with care and respect; from now, so shall I!"

Mochanna looked over his shoulder and smiled knowingly.

Grimbald continued, "I have remembered everything you have told me since we first met, and more, master."

Mochanna simply said, "Eat." And ladle out a bowl of broth for his student.

Both student and master held out their bowls at arm's length in harmony and bowed their heads in gratitude for their fare.

As soon as they finished their meals, Mochanna said, "Now do your chores, and we will teach you about mortal combat, but firstly without weapons."

Grimbald looked on surprised, scratching his head but at the same time fully accepting his master's direction.

After his chores, Grimbald went with Mochanna into a clearing. Mochanna stood for a moment sniffing the air like a dog and cupping his ears with his hands, walking slowly in a circle. Grimbald worked out that he was smelling the air for the presence of any humankind in the vicinity and listening for their voices. "Are you satisfied that we will be undisturbed, master?" asked Grimbald.

"For the time being, young man," his master replied with a quick grin.

Mochanna had brought a sack full of items along with a spear. Again, the boy held his tongue as he realised that he would be the one unarmed!

The wizard first brought out a neat replica sword made of wood and walked toward Grimbald slowly with the sword pointing to his face. "What shall I do now?" asked Mochanna.

Grimbald was now less certain of his master's intentions, "Strike me... I suppose?" he responded.

"If I did so, then where do you think I would strike?" asked Mochanna.

Suddenly he could make out what his master was thinking... "You will strike me in the side of the leg, a cutting blow that would impair my ability to fight."

Mochanna was slightly taken aback by his apprentice's remark. "You have mastered one thing I did not expect so soon, young man. I will have to be on my guard. Be warned, though; this is not possible with everyone, which is where your instincts and observations must be at their peak.

Always take note of how a person walks. Are they light on their feet? Do they walk from the hip? A sign that someone uses their back for strength. Do they take long strides? It can mean someone who is impatient and at the same if they take short quick strides. You must know your enemy as well as you can, simply by the way they move. Look also for the weaknesses in their stride. The manner in which they look at you is often times a mask. If they have no fear or uncertainty about you, they do not have to show an angry face. So, the one who shows no feeling is the one you should be wary of!"

Grimbald felt at that moment everything was falling into place; events and practices were starting to weld into his every fibre. He suddenly started to shake as if being throttled, his eyes became red, and his head felt like it would burst open. He was at once afraid and simultaneously in some kind of masochistic ecstasy.

Mochanna was, once more, surprised to see what was happening with his young disciple.

Grimbald had absorbed the guidance of special forces. Mochanna could feel what had happened and knew who it was that now guided the young man. As much as he knew that Grimbald had some connection with him, he had not realised how close.

The wizard put his student through his paces with a wide variety of practices in combat from different nations. The day passed quickly. Apart from a short mid-day interval, they hadn't stopped, and achingly tired as he was, Grimbald yearned for more. The only drawback at that time was his sudden sadness for his family.

Mochanna picked up on this and decided to explain the situation to him in a simplistic manner. "I know how you feel, young man, but know this. You had the benefit of a good family, and not many can say that. You have good memories to cherish, wits, good health, and potential above many who have gone before or shall come after you. Everything happens for a reason, Grimbald... that is the Way of Wyrd."

That evening, Mochanna baked a fish with fresh bread, herbs, and wild garlic and asked his student, as usual, to say thank you for the life that would now sustain him.

Grimbald had come to truly realise what Myrte had meant about the honour and privilege of learning from his master.

The following day was almost a repeat of the previous day's programme but with the added incentive of unarmed combat, in which Mochanna was particularly skilled.

"If you are surrounded in a woodland by several men of varying ability, knowing what you do about their presence and movement. What would your response be?" asked Mochanna.

Grimbald was almost about to enter the mind of his master but realised that he would be caught out if his response would sound clever or Mochanna-like. Instead, he searched in himself as quickly as he could and offered, "I would firstly see if I could ally myself to them and their cause in order to gain greater opportunity to escape. Or I might run and hopefully fox them with my moves. Or I could bluff them about hidden forces at my disposal?"

Mochanna summed up: "Well done, young man, for not doing what you first thought of... intruding my thoughts!

I quite like the first idea. If you could see some kind of insignia or emblem you were familiar with, it is likely you would get away with that. The second notion is always a good one, to run if you feel you could have the advantage. But if you should try the one about hidden forces, you would need to have something else hidden up your sleeve."

No sooner than those words left Mochanna's lips, a young girl's voice came out of the nearby forest, calling, "Grimbald, Grimbald... here... here."

Grimbald looked in the direction he thought the voice was coming from, but his instincts told him all was not right. He knew instantly it was not a spirit and turned to look at his master. Mochanna smiled and opened his mouth just enough to send out this strange female-sounding voice, without moving his lips and tongue, "Come Grimbald... find me."

Grimbald was frozen with astonishment and asked fearfully, "How do you do that, master? It is so strange; I could swear it is coming from the forest. Is this... something else I must learn?"

"I think you should, young man. It has saved me from many awkward moments and can be the soothing antidote to a suffering soul. It is one talent that should not go underestimated. In fact, there are many skills that you shall acquire which will outwit your foes and help your allies through sleight of hands and image manipulation, all of which I hope you will keep secret, wholly to yourself."

Mochanna sat, continuing to lecture, the boy enthralled. "The mind and the body are vessels for you to fill for the benefit of all others, including yourself. You must never feel you have learned enough, never think highly of yourself no matter what flattery comes your way, and never be complacent. That would be your worst indulgence, given who you are becoming and, one day, will be. You have been blessed with great abilities; treat them with utmost reverence. They are loaned to you, so prove your right to own them. If you do not use them, they will wither and separate themselves from you, as they did from your mother and grandfather." Grimbald looked a little surprised though he always had a strange feeling about his mother and much more so of her father. "If you do as I do, and live as simply as possible, there will be no distractions from your improvement or betterment."

"I do know that you will go in search of your sister and will be distracted from your true purpose. For myself, I believe I have no family any longer, bar one, but I shall not speak of him for now. Be always on your guard and listen to the spirits. We shall retire for today, but you must ready yourself for your part in the coming war." Mochanna got up and playfully threw a staff in Grimbald's face, which he caught easily.

"There, master, I was ready," exclaimed Grimbald.

The wizard immediately spun around, grabbed Grimbald by the hair, put one foot behind his ankle, and pulled the boy to the floor. "No, my boy, you suddenly became complacent," he uttered.

CHAPTER SEVENTEEN

The Hidden Evil

Wenslau was more than ready to help his new guest; there appeared to be something in him that Wenslau admired and respected, maybe a reflection of himself. He had an inkling that there was something to learn from the stranger, and Wenslau was never too proud not to admit he could still learn from someone. "I will send three of my best men to help you find these wormy scum... but could you tell me what events brought you to my door? What transpired which tormented you?" he asked over a beaker of mulled wine, as the pair sat in front of the roaring fire, crackling, and hissing from the snow, occasionally falling down the chimney.

"I can, sire… about four days ago, two of my close friends and me were called to help in a dispute between two landowners, one wealthy man and one, shall we say, a little humbler. The humbler man was of a dubious character but had everyone believe he was a victim of the wealthy man's fancy. As soon as I met the little man, I knew. The worst of this man's habits was the company he kept, people of no moral presence or bearing. We had been sent by a friend of a friend to ascertain what was the truth of this situation?"

"I have to ask?" enquired Wenslau. "Who is the man to whom you did his bidding, and who are the other two? I already have my suspicions."

"You may know them all, sire. The lord for whom I worked is Coenedd of Wick, some six days ride from here, I would say. He is a respected and powerful man of mixed birth, half Pict and half Saxon, like your wife, sire. He and I became good friends after fighting against each other in a border war. Suffice it to say we have helped each other in many ways, and one of his close friends was facing a possible loss of his lands and possessions if the local Reeve should decide in the other's favour. My two companions and I were to enquire what events had taken place to bring about such misrepresentations. A war was something neither party could afford."

"Nay, I know nothing of this Coenedd," remarked Wenslau.

"You shall come to."

Wenslau raised an eyebrow.

"As part of our investigation, we decided to follow a small party of men... filthy, horrible men you could smell half a mile away on a soft breeze. They were mostly hooded but naked around the legs, which were yellowed and scarred. They rode horses without any reins, bridles, or saddlery. We decided to portray as if we didn't know each other; thus, we kept some distance. After around twelve miles or so, we saw the men arriving at their homestead. It was a fortified place mainly built of stone; left from Roman's time, I believe, Horeden, that was it. It was almost in ruins, with dotted wooden buildings and mainly women folk at work in the yards. We pretended to be traders in arms with our store in the nearby town of Dunholm. We would ask for directions and hope for an offer of food or an overnight stay. But we did not bargain for what was to come... I was angry with myself for not being alert enough, for my complacency. This is why I rage inside; those men could still be alive..." tears started to well in his eyes.

There was a sudden rustle toward the stable door as Eudda came through to find Aedric trying to listen in to the conversation. Aedric blushed as Eudda asked him why he was there and what he was doing.

"E-r-r, I... I... I... was just about to call on the master when I noticed he was talking to our guest, so I... I held back a little."

Eudda brushed past Aedric, giving him a scornful look, confident in her mistress's remarks about looking after her no matter what. She had no idea she was going to play a powerful role in the future of this household.

Wenslau was a little deaf, but Grimbald heard Aedric and Eudda quite clearly, prompting him to whisper to Wenslau. "It may not be my place to say, sire, but I sense you may have a weasel in your midst, someone who pretends to be what he is not, and I believe you have had your doubts for some time?"

"Aye, tis so. I am determined to find the truth of this man," whispered Wenslau, adding, "It was only last week when one of my maids reported seeing him talking to that snake of a monk… Barnard, he is called? There have been quite a number of nasty rumours about that one. I think the Abbot is probably a good man by all accounts, but his second was born among the snakes if all they say is true of him.

WELL?"

Aedric came forward with a feeble excuse, in a sycophantic manner, about Grimbald's horse recovering well and starting to eat normally, saying what an excellent steed he was.

Grimbald stared into the fire, disgusted by the presence of the manservant. He could already sense this man's inner thoughts and his full scheme.

"Please continue," asked Wenslau after harshly dismissing Aedric.

"Well, my close friend Uhtric offered to go ahead of myself and Cenric, Uhtric's half-brother. He would say that we were delayed by demonstrating new weapons, recently delivered. The evening light was fading by the time we arrived, and Uhtric was already enjoying himself with a local wench and some wine in a shabby tavern in the square. There were only three other men in the place when we entered, looking rather like the ones we followed; I could not be sure. Uhtric seemed as if he'd already drunk enough to think properly.

Cenric and I asked for ale, thinking the wine must be a little too strong. We spoke to each other, somewhat confused as to why no one had asked who we were or why we had come. We surmised it was probably some kind of large hostelry, so we asked one of the girls, by which time Cenric and I were suddenly feeling the worse for drinking. We agreed it must be that we hadn't eaten since early morn and should acquire sustenance.

The scruffy girl looked very shy when she replied that it was a hostelry for cattle and sheep drovers; we agreed it made sense. By the time our food arrived, Uhtric was asleep at the table, and we were dozing. My suspicions suddenly aroused, though, as the three men got up and moved toward us. Cenric was by this time as helpless as his brother. I, being the one more conscious, was delivered a hard blow to the chin, but rather than knocking me out, it brought back my senses a tad. However, I managed to let them think the opposite, hoping to be able to put up a fight a little later. As I was so weary, it was difficult to make out where we were being taken, and there wasn't much light…"

"By the gods, man… what were they about?" begged Wenslau.

146

Grimbald continued, "I remember, although everything seemed blurry, they removed our swords and weaponry. They then dragged us through some sort of kitchen whereupon I felt sick at the sight of animal and human carcasses, dismembered men, women, and children. Limbs and heads strewn about the place, with the sight and smell of blood everywhere. Despite all that, there were two people fornicating in the corridor, near to where we were deposited, no doubt twas what they deemed acceptable.

In truth, sire, I fear they may have been cannibals. Descriptions of this type have been told to me before. I vaguely remember one of their kind eating a human heart fresh from the body like it was an apple or ripened fruit.

In a moment, we were all thrown into a small cellar with no door, where a tiny amount of light shone in from a beacon in the square. The blood started to race in my whole body, and I realised that it was only going to be me to survive as I had neither the strength nor the time or ability to look out for my friends.

I managed to smell the air to reach the stables and sensed my horse, Aylmer, was distressed."

Wenslau looked confused.

"He helped me to his direction. But I had, while escaping, to fool and fight off a few of my captors. Luckily I found some weaponry in the stable where Aylmer was kept with some spare clothing. They had even tried to get him drunk and had bitten into his face.   I was bitterly cold but so thankful the snow started to fall; it soon turned into a blizzard. I knew they were not far behind me, but my senses were keen enough to gain some distance between us. I rode with a desperation I had never felt before. Aylmer took no persuading, as he wanted out of that place as much as I did. My instincts brought me here. The rest, as you know, is my good fortune upon landing at your door. I do not know how long I travelled, but would soon remember the way!"

Wenslau observed, "The snows are early for the time of year, but they have no doubt aided your luck. We must talk some more, my man, but I grow hungry and need some fine food and beer in my belly." He smiled broadly and patted Grimbald on the shoulder, rising stiffly from his chair, saying, "Come, before we eat, I have something to show you."

Wenslau led Grimbald down to the stables, passing all the geese, cattle, and goats, then into a chamber at the very back, where a huge, padlocked door, set into the rock, faced them. Grimbald sensed Wenslau's excitement as he unlocked the heavy wooden door. "Eich made this especially for me! Now young man... what do you think of this?" he lit a torch with a flint-flick. The room was low and very wide, quite warm, but it was full of weaponry, some new, some old, and some ancient. It was like a museum, well ordered for Wenslau, and all items were in immaculate condition, gleaming in the flickering light.

"We stand beneath the hearth, as you may feel the heat so that I may keep them all in the finest fettle. There are only a handful of people who know what this room is for, and only two of my most trusted men look after this place, Esmond and Haydn. You are the only stranger I have shown this collection to, but I have a strong feeling we have each other's trust."

Grimbald nodded, eyes wide open; he recognised a few weapons Mochanna had introduced him to and surprised his host with his knowledge of them. Wenslau was quite impressed.

"Ah, what about these? Do you know of them?" asked Wenslau, pointing to an assembly of Persian knives. "Although I have these handsome knives, I would have to say, I still prefer my seaxa!" he added, holding onto his knife firmly.

"M-m-m… Let me feel them, and I may be able to tell you," said Grimbald, adding after a short pause, "These four are ceremonial. These two belonged to warrior kings or princes, but the long one, like a sword, belonged to some kind of strange man who looked after many royal women. He was not quite a man… a Euchar or something like that?" He halted and whispered. "Say nothing, sire; your weasel is down here. I sense him at the entrance to the byre!"

Wenslau whispered through gritted teeth, "I will skin this man alive."

"Be patient, sire, as this man will be of more use to us alive with the help of your Spanish maid," Grimbald suggested.

Wenslau looked on a little confused as Grimbald went ahead, he locked the heavy door, and they made their way back through the stables.

The young warrior had just surprised himself with his capabilities and how much was being revealed to him. *There had been so much lacking in him of late,* he thought. Too many mistakes had been made. He was starting to get a little restless now, wanting to pursue his tormentors and assassins of his friends, but in his head, a voice was telling him to stay put. "All will come together."

CHAPTER EIGHTEEN

The Humble Man

Several miles south of Wenslau's village was a recently built abbey and servants' village by the name of Coverham. The abbey, having been established seven years ago, was now more of a permanent structure. The larger part of the village was within the walls of the abbey.

Christian influence was very well established in most of the southern half of Northanhymbra, and much of what happened in Coverham took its lead from Eorforwic. Coverham abbey was headed by an abbot by the name of Wilhelm, a very devoted Christian with high standards, particularly for himself. His second was Father Barnardo, who preferred to be called Barnard so as to Anglicise himself. He had a slightly different notion of how the church and its followers should be run. Barnardo came from a very oppressed background in Northern Iberia, a strong Basque family who were very poor and gave their youngest child, seven years old, to the church just in order to survive. For that, he would never forgive his parents for abandoning him or have anything to do with them ever again. The young man grew up with a bitter streak that would never leave him, deciding that all he ever wanted was power and status; let no one stand in his way.

Coverham was a bustling town when Grimbald arrived on his third day as Wenslau's guest. He was accompanied by Inga, Bronwen, and Aelfswip - one of Bronwen's maids. Grimbald rode his much-recovered steed alongside the cart with family and maid. It was a cold but bright, sunny day with heavy rolling clouds in the west. The recent snow had all but cleared. There were all kinds of scents in the air, vegetables, meat, live fowl, sheep, and cattle, all to be sold in the market.

For the most part, Coverham had a good feeling about it, homely and friendly. But not long after coming through the gates of the abbey and village, an incident occurred. Coming out of the main abbey doors, two men, one small and thin, covering his head with his arms, a servant. The other man was medium-sized, having exceptionally broad shoulders, an oblong face, and vivid blue-green eyes. His beard was long and sandy, with a mop of coarse light brown hair shaved around the crown. He wore a pale brown tunic with a gold embroidered belt, befitting his status, and walked with a slight stoop, constantly looking round from his deep brow. By his side, he carried a long staff.

Aelfswip quickly pointed in reverence with a loud whisper, "Look 'tis Father Barnard, madam."

Grimbald had been busy looking in the other direction at the market traders, half daydreaming if he would one day find his sister. Yet knowing the time may be a little further off than he would wish. The ladies all gasped as Barnard swiftly hit the servant across the face, knocking him to the floor and chastising him for being in the wrong place at the wrong time. The monk gave a cursory, couldn't care less look in the direction of Bronwen and others, latterly nodding toward Grimbald in a so what manner?

Two of the abbeys' young monks came out of the abbey shortly afterwards and asked Barnard to return for some important matter.

"So that was the renowned monk," declared Grimbald.

Bronwen just nodded as Inga said, "Horriblest man ever!"

Aelfswip countered, "Maybe we have caught him on a bad day, or the other man might have been very bad?"

Inga and Bronwen looked at each other and shook their heads. Aelfswip was not the brightest of maids.

Marching down the main hall of the abbey cloisters, his staff tamping the floor with every other step, strode the cold Barnard in his stiff, heavily made sandals. His face was about to change expression like a cloud passing the sun to greet Father Wilhelm and report daily affairs. He stood for a second as the monks attending the huge doors opened to admit him into the *Chamber of Commerce*, as

Wilhelm liked to call it. Barnard smiled a sickly smile, with which the Abbot was all too accustomed.

"Well Father, be we solvent and with armies of followers this day?" The balding abbot quipped through bushy, brown eyebrows as he was half reading a report.

"I am afraid a little of neither, Your Reverence. We are, in actuality, more than solvent, having just this day acquired a gift of some fifteen hectares of land to the west from one of our local lairds in his last will. But as for the armies of followers, I fear we may number slightly too few," replied Barnard in a deep gravelly voice.

"Oh well, no doubt the land brings with it a few followers who may be tied to it. See if there is ought of subsequence, Barnard?" ordered the abbot in his usually mild tone.

Behind Wilhelm were three monks with their backs turned, all working at desks. Two were writing, and one, Garaint, was transcribing ogham scripts and symbols he had collected over many years. The abbot had commissioned him because he was curious about the land's history. They were so sparse, and much of what had been written seemed like gibberish. He half turned toward Barnard's voice but thought better of it. Garaint had an intense dislike for Barnard for many reasons, but the main one was the death of one of the novices, covered up by Barnard's lackeys. Garaint, himself, had been previously accused of murder and, because of the uncertainty of events, was advised to either take to the cloth or be a slave to an evil squire. He was intelligent and enquiring but prone to being foolhardy, one of the reasons he came to be where he was.

At the market in Coverham, Grimbald decided to buy some herbs as his stocks were low, and he didn't believe he would have time to forage, as events were taking place at an unprecedented rate. Quite a few people stared at him with his distinct hair plaits, being taller than average, and his unusual weaponry. Two of the abbey's soldiers decided to ask what he was doing in the area. Before either of the men could speak, Grimbald turned toward the men and said with a gentle smile, "I am a guest of Lord Wenslau and accompanying his ladyfolk on their errands. Does this satisfy your curiosity, sirs?" The two men looked at each other, a little puzzled. One of them just patted Grimbald on the arm in a friendly manner and smiled in return as they then walked off.

Inga was so impressed with Grimbald. *How calm and brave he is,* she thought, standing with mouth half open.

"Close your mouth and your thoughts," said her mother. "We have many things to buy today, and we must try and get the late bargains."

"Why, mother, why do we always do that? We have enough money to buy what and when we want," asked Inga, embarrassed due to Grimbald's presence.

"Your Father insists… you should know that! He doesn't think we should spend unnecessarily. It was the way his folk taught him."

Grimbald grinned at them both, putting his hand on the back of Inga's head, saying, "Nought is wrong in that young lady."

Inga was not too pleased at him placing his hand on her head but liked being described as a young lady. Bronwen distinctly disapproved of such flattery.

As the market was about to close, Grimbald had been going back and forth with the goods while Aelfswip sat guarding the cart and wares. A group of soldiers came toward them. Grimbald had an inkling of what was going on and simply tended his horse. About thirty feet away stood Barnard, near the main doors again and looking on.

One small soldier leading the group, full of confidence with his entourage, suggested that Grimbald might be a wanted man from a nearby town.

Grimbald walked straight up to the man and said, "Which town, by what name is this man known to you, what is he wanted for, who else knows this man, does he have family in the locality, and who instructed you to approach me?"

The man gulped and stuttered, completely bamboozled by the tirade of questions, "W... w... we... well, I am not able to divulge my commander's name b... b... but w... w... we c... c... could be w... w... wrong. Y... y... you are somewhat p... p... presumptuous, sir."

"Nay, sir, I am simply being honest and direct over other people's presumptions about myself," came the prompt reply.

The little man turned toward his group, who all seemed to shrug their shoulders at the warrior's reply. Suddenly he marched off toward the rear of the abbey. Barnard looked on, shaking his head at the little man's incompetence, disappointed the situation didn't escalate.

This was the first time Aelfswip had seen the other side of Barnard, and she was quite upset by his actions. She knew he had a reputation for being strict, but she hadn't bargained on him being devious and cruel.

Grimbald, meanwhile, had made a comprehensive estimation of Barnard and his workings. There was a deep-seated dread within him of what might become of his host, the family, and the people with whom he was connected. He knew this would be one of the most complicated tasks set before him. Firstly, he would have to convince Wenslau of what they were about to face.

Just as the family was about to leave the abbey grounds, a very pleasant little man appeared from out of a side door to the abbey. He was slightly ruddy-faced with neatly combed, thinning brown hair with bushy eyebrows and seemed to constantly wear half a pinched smile. Scurrying towards the market, he was soon surrounded by villagers and traders alike.

"Your Holiness, can I help?" asked one man from the market. People all around started genuflecting and crossing themselves, most of them offering their help or something of value.

"What are you doing, Your Reverence?" cried one of the soldiers.

The abbot wondered about enjoying his brief freedom. "No, no, no, I solely wanted to buy some apples from the market. I would like to do something normal. Bless you, child, and you good man and you…"

Barnard was swiftly on the scene with his henchmen forcing people back. "Your Reverence, you are just not safe to be amongst these commoners; who knows what should become of you?" Barnard was sick of saying the same thing, for it was not the first time. He revelled in controlling the masses with force and keeping his master under control.

"We are all the same, all God's creatures!" insisted Wilhelm as he was escorted back to the abbey.

Witnessing this event, Grimbald thought, *therein lies the pity; the good and humble man is more a puppet than a leader. Too often 'tis so.*

The group seized the opportunity to make for home.

CHAPTER NINETEEN

The Delicate Plan

It was Grimbald's third day as Wenslau's guest, and he was starting to grow impatient about following up on the perpetrators of his friend's murders. He was up early before the servants could prepare the morning fest. Aylmer, Grimbald's horse, was recovering well and seemed to enjoy the new smells and surroundings as they exercised by the river. The knight surveyed the land and people at almost every turn. *A busy village compared to many!* he mused. As he neared the outer edges of the village, Aylmer grew skittish and began to pull away from the river. Grimbald soon discovered why, as the edges of the bank were splattered with blood on the remaining snow. Skirting further behind gorse bushes were two young bodies, with two pails on a yoke close by them. The young man and girl, side by side, had been brutally bludgeoned to death.

Grimbald dismounted and told Ceadda to stay put. Crouching beside the bodies, he first laid his hand over the young man's brow and tried to read his mind to learn more about the events that took place. Then, he did the same with the girl. Immediately his eyes were drawn to the other side of the bank. Many images flashed through his mind as he tried to set his attention on the offenders some mile or two away. But something was telling him all of the recent events were somehow linked. First, he must meet with Wenslau and appraise him of the situation. They have to come up with a plan to tackle the circumstances.

Looking at the bodies once more, Grimbald rode to the nearest house to the river. He tied Aylmer to the fence. Before he even neared the house, out came two dogs, one medium-sized and feisty, the other large but thin, probably used for hunting deer. A well-wrapped tall woman made a cursory glance out of the door, swiftly followed by the man of the house.

"Hail there, what be you about, sir?" asked the man, suddenly recognising the visitor. "Ah! Tis Grimbald, is it not, Wenslau's guest?"

"Aye, it is… I have some bad news, I fear. Esmond is it not?" the man nodded. "There are two young bodies down by the river; they have been set upon by at least three men. They are a girl and a boy."

Esmond's wife rushed out at hearing the news.

"Wait, let me go," insisted Esmond, looking very worried.

The two men went over to the bodies. Esmond gasped and spluttered, tears welling up in his eyes. Aebba, his wife, had followed closely behind and let out a deep, soulful gasp, unable to breathe, and collapsed to her knees beside their daughter's body, sobbing violently.

"It is our Ealdgyd," said Esmond, fighting back the tears. "And young Hama, the Wheelwright's son."

"They were in love with each other!" stated Grimbald.

"They were, but my wife did not want them to be together. She was promised to a wealthy cousin of hers," Esmond's voice trembled... "I just wanted for her to be happy, but the gods have decided to punish us for some reason."

"If she had done as I had told her, this would not have happened!" screamed Aebba in fury, tears and snot running down her face as she wiped them away with her sleeve and shawl.

Grimbald disapproved strongly of Aebba's ideas of betrothal but held his tongue and rebuked out of respect.

Soon half the village had come to see what had happened. Soon Wenslau visited the place, riding Greymoon. "Esmond, my good man, I am so heavy of heart with great sorrow for you and your wife. I have just heard what has happened. Why would anyone take the lives of these two innocents? I am sensing there are sinister connivances being played against us. A callous murder of these two innocent youths. Does Algar know of his son?" A sudden silence... "Then someone better hurry and tell him.

Dreda, you were a friend of his wife before she passed; perhaps you should go?" he said, nodding to a stout woman just behind him.

"Aye, sire, that I will," she replied with great urgency and scurried off to the east of the village.

A few of the women joined Aebba, trying to comfort her, and some crying along with her.

The murder prompted a discussion in Wenslau's household. Grimbald insisted that no servant should be around for what he was about to say. Wenslau had an intense sense of faith in him. He acknowledged him as very wise, someone worthy of taking advice from.

Grimbald began to talk quietly as the fire crackled and the lights flickered in the room from occasional draughts. Inga was asked if she would go to help Eudda for a trip into Coverham the next morning as there were items Bronwen would like to sell... things that some of the poorer people might want to buy.

Holding a piece of charcoal in his hand, Grimbald decided to draw some of his plans on the flagstone floor near the fire.

It had been a long night for Wenslaus' family, well past their usual hour to retire. All but Grimbald were exhausted, who had renewed vigour. Bronwen was perplexed by how much Grimbald seemed to know of the area, having only been with them such a short time, and how well he seemed to know the people he so briefly met.

Wenslau gave out instructions as he usually did before going to his bed. Aedric had just brought newly cleaned leathers and outwear for his master from another servant's station to be placed on clothes rails by Wenslau's chamber when Eudda suddenly bumped into him coming out of the doorway.

"Oh, I do apologise," she said in a sweet tone.

Aedric was a little taken aback by her manner and thought maybe she wasn't so bad after all, though not entirely sure. He just smiled a sickly smile and said jokily, "Out of the dark comes light!"

Eudda smiled politely and went on her busy way.

The following morning a cart of goods, some fine and some not-so-fine clothes, were taken to the market at Little Coverham village not far from the abbey to sell. In actual fact, Little Coverham was far larger than the abbey village and held a much bigger market for people from miles around. Many well-known faces would be there, and many fortunes could be won or lost in its inns. Intervillage battles would often be fought owing to the recklessness of some of the younger hierarchy. Wenslau had only ever been there once and decided never to go again. "Too many worm-heads," he declared.

Wenslau told Aedric he wanted him to go to the market to seek out the silver smith, as he wanted to reward Esmond for all his years of good service with fine regalia for his horse. And he was to take Eudda to find a fine dress for Esmond's wife. Aelfswip, one of Bronwen's maids, another manservant, and a young girl from Wenslau's village were to go also, to set up and sell her clothes. Aside from that, Wenslau asked if there were any shepherd boys with sheep for sale to ensure they were not just slave boys and to bring them back with a full cart. "I think after some advisement we should try rearing sheep. Many of our neighbours farm them. They have become most popular, and I do like the meat." he said to Bronwen as she rolled her eyes with a whatever-next expression.

Aedric was slightly unsure of suddenly having to be with Eudda for so long after just cooling the waters somewhat, although he did have a modicum of respect for her directness. "Anyway," he told himself, "it will only be for the journey." And he thought he wouldn't want to be burdened with the ever-prattling Aelfswip on his own. Not long after the wagon and its passengers left for Little Coverham, another figure left the village, rather scruffy and leading a jenny with empty baskets. The figure was stooped and breathing heavily from his hooded face.

Eudda had not said anything for the most part of the journey; in fact, she wasn't allowed to, as Aelfswip never stopped since leaving Wenslau's leigh. Aedric decided to drum up the conversation and ask Eudda a little about her history. Although he wasn't conspicuously interested, she knew it. Eudda told how she came from the north of Iberia, from the Basque country, and that she had been kidnapped to be sold as a slave when she was only six years old. And that she was nearly fourteen summers when Aedric's predecessor bought him; he was a kind man, she added.

"Aye, what did take him... some kind of canker, was it not?" asked Aedric.

"Well, we're not sure if it was the canker, some kind of poison, or the wicker woman who treated him. I would never have gone to her," Eudda said sadly.

"I know, I would not trust the woman either. She seemed to take the money and scurry away. I think she did not have the skill or knowledge to minister medicaments," he agreed.

The two carried on occasionally talking as they were nearing the village, struggling to hear each other over Aelfswip's ramblings, even after Aedric had insisted several times for her to be quiet with the threat of a stick.

There were heavy grey clouds about, and a little touch of humidity in the air, plus the flies were gathering more around the heads of the packhorses.

"I do believe it will rain," said Eudda.

"Even I would say that, to be fair certain," replied Aedric, upon whose very words, bullets of heavy, icy rain suddenly bounced on and around them, lifting the drying soil and flattening the sleepy grasses. A mixed blessing for the horses. They scurried into the village, tethering the cobs and gathering under the wagon cover, waiting for the weather to break a little. Aelfswip was extremely uncomfortable being so close to Aedric. The other servant, Thomas, offered to cover the horses, but Aedric, in his usual cursory manner, said to leave them.

About twenty yards away, the figure that was following on the bridge was tying up his jenny, his body half turned from sight. The man was slightly bandy-legged and shuffled, having endured many years of hard toil and travel. He appeared to speak to jenny and then headed in the direction of the market carrying a large canvas shoulder bag and a staff.

"I will go find the silversmith woman," Aedric said to Eudda in his clumsy way, always of the opinion that women would never be quite equal of a man. "If you would go and find the tailor. Order what you will for the master. I will meet you here at the onset of dusk," he scurried away with haste and purpose.

"Tis fine with me, sir," replied Eudda, marching off with Aelfswip close behind.

"You will have to stay with the wagon and horses, Thomas," said Aelfswip as she trotted after Eudda. "I'll bring you some freshly cooked pork skins and fresh midday bread if I can," she added.

The main road into the village was getting very busy by mid-morning, and a small troupe of Huscarls from the abbey were part of the crowd. In the middle was a familiar and formidable figure, Barnard. He wore a large, brimmed hat with heavy grey robes, having a large, rather fanciful cross and chain on his chest. His first mission was to visit the largest of the local taverns that always kept a stock of his favourite wine. Occasionally it would be paid for, but only when Barnard cared to. The innkeeper didn't mind too much, as his men would spend quite a lot on ale, as did many of Barnard's sycophants also.

Just south of the main market square, Eudda ordered finery from the tailors, having used Aelfswip as the model, owing to her similar size and stature to Aebba. As Eudda came from the shop, the figure she saw earlier brushed past her, grunted, and stamped his staff hard on the cobbles as if to say look where you are going.

Aelfswip was angered by the man's actions and abused him for being bad-spirited. Eudda made light of it suddenly, saying, "I think we should visit the church as we are here to pray for the peace and healing of Esmond and Aebba's hearts. They are, after all, the main reason we are here this day." Aelfswip agreed wholeheartedly, as she just loved churches and the whole idea of them.

As Eudda and Aelfswip approached the church, they caught sight of Aedric near the entrance talking to Father Barnard. The ladies both bowed their heads as they neared.

"Ah, Your Reverence, this one of my lady's senior maids, Eudda," said Aedric with his authoritarian air, completely ignoring Aelfswip. "She hails from the same part of the world as yourself, I believe?"

Barnard threw his head back a little, "Is that so?" he asked, seeming none too pleased.

"I believe we may come from the same parts, Father," Eudda replied, feeling somewhat unsure of herself.

Barnard asked several questions, where her village was and what her father did etc., in his old mother tongue just to be sure. She replied straight away in slightly clumsy Basque and surprised Barnard with her intellect. Aedric was also impressed. Aelfswip just stood with her mouth wide open, suddenly remembering to buy Thomas his bread and roast pork skins.

"That is the first time in many years I have spoken the old language… and the first time I've enjoyed the experience," remarked the priest.

"And me too, Father," replied Eudda, submissively adding, "I must apologise for my limited memory of our language…"

Barnard interrupted, "We must do this again sometime. Now you must go; I have business to attend to!" Issuing a knowing look to Aedric as they both turned toward the rear of the church. Aedric waved his hand for the women to go back to the wagon.

As Eudda was leading towards the narrow street ahead, a lone shabby, hooded figure stood in the distance, looking straight in her direction. Adjusting his shoulder bag and stamping his staff, he hobbled off into the crowds and disappeared.

Out of the blue, Aedric came back running, grabbing Eudda by the arm, startling her and Aelfswip, looking flustered. "I had almost forgotten," he said, slightly out of breath, "We must seek out the sheep for our master." He pushed a small purse of money into her hand and told her that it should be enough to purchase what was required. "I will be with you directly," he finished.

Late that afternoon, the shopping party trundled back into the dusky village with their newly acquired shepherd boy, twenty sheep, and a sheepdog following behind the wagon. The boy was skinny and tall, with a mop of brown curly hair, carrying a crook, and was, without doubt, a competent shepherd, anticipating the sheep's every move, with his dog acting in unison.

Wenslau came from the house to greet them. He asked the boy his name, but all he could understand was that the boy's name was Gruffydd. The boy's Kournwahle accent was so strong he couldn't tell what else the lad was saying. Fumbling to understand the boy, Wenslau immediately summoned his head stockman to see to the shepherd and asked him to make sure the boy was well-fed and watered.

Coming soon after, Grimbald appeared from the stables with a wink and smiled at Wenslau. Wenslau raised his brow in a single nod.

CHAPTER TWENTY

Deception

ater that same week, Frigsdaeg to be exact, Eudda was organising the laundry for servants and workers, as well as those for the household. She and another servant, Hildred, were busy making soap when Aedric suddenly appeared in the doorway and beckoned Eudda over for a quiet word.

"You have brought a little light into someone's world, young lass!" remarked Aedric.

"What do you mean?" said Eudda rather puzzled.

"I think you know, and it is of great import that I ask you to attend him as soon as you are free to do so. I see a great man who has need of some diversion … nothing untoward, I hasten to add. The Holy Father is suitably impressed by you and your countenance. He said he would like the comfort of speaking once more in his mother tongue with you. (His head was moving around as he whispered in Eudda's ear) There could be some remuneration if you are happy to be of service, I believe?"

"The mistress and I are to attend the service on Sonnandaeg. Perhaps I can make some time as she likes to socialise with friends near the abbey?" Eudda suggested nervously.

"I shall inform his holiness," said Aedric.

"What did that Sheiss want?" asked Hildred as Eudda returned to her duties. Hildred was a tad foul-mouthed about everything and everyone and a rather masculine woman, too, quite intimidating to her colleagues.

"Oh, it was nought. He merely wanted to know if I needed any more materials for the laundering as he was going into Coverham," she replied rather unconvincingly.

Hildred tutted and just said, "Aye!" sarcastically.

Soon a flurry of youths, boys and girls of varying ages, were ushered in from the fields, ordered to clean their shoes at the doorway, strip, and throw their dirty clothes into the corner of the room. The boys with their tub of warm water and the girls with theirs. They were then told to wash each other with soapy mosses in the tubs and dry with warm cloths before sitting for their supper. All was regimented, and Hildred delighted in having it so; no chatter or giggling or questions asked. Their treatment was quite generous for serfs, but Bronwen insisted it should be, as a newly recruited Christian, though she really *sat on both sides of the fence.*

Early the next day, the sun was just rising as Luuah came up from the river with freshly caught fish for morning fest. As he was passing Wenslau's byre, he saw Grimbald seated near the door, facing the sun, cross-legged, hands in a praying position and in some kind of trance. Luuah understood quite well what was happening and laid one of the fish he had caught next to Grimbald's feet, wrapping it in some dried, horse-chestnut leaves he would always carry in his sack. The young warrior was connecting with his former guide and master, Mochanna, whom he deemed to be not very far away. The communication was vague and limited but poignant enough to help Grimbald with his quest. He felt a surge of serene warmth over his whole body, and as he opened his eyes, he looked down at his feet and burst into a great fit of laughter. "Who else could that be?" he said to himself. Grimbald then promised himself to go later, talk and say thanks to the eccentric Pict.

Some days later, in a small room at the rear of Coverham Abbey, Barnard surrounded himself with a coven of men, all listening intensely to his instructions. Four of the men were very smelly and shabby, standing a distance from the others. The men took their orders and left after a short time, looking at each other for fear of their secret being exposed. As they walked out of the door, there was Aedric waiting for his reward from the priest for the given information. Just as Aedric was entering the chamber, Brother Garaint passed at the end of the corridor and heard Barnard's gravelly voice, ushering the man in. Tempted as he was to try and listen at the door, he cautioned himself about such deviance that may undo him. He did, however, resolve to remain in the vicinity with the hope of discovering something important, suspicious of some sort of deception. His patience was about to be rewarded after an uncomfortable wait. Two of the abbey guards knocked on Barnard's door, with Eudda alongside them. The door was pushed open, and Eudda was told to wait as Barnard and Aedric continued with their conversation in the corridor.

Barnard's final whisperings being, "And remember, tomorrow we instigate our plan. Make sure the young warrior is distracted away. I rely on you to play your part, make good on it, and I shall reward you well!" He was loud enough to be overheard as voices were easily carried in the corridors.

Garaint had heard talk of this new young warrior lodging with Wenslau. *He could be the only one they were speaking about,* he thought. Barnard went back to the study and joined in conversation once more with Eudda. This time he was more enquiring of her master's household, but she smiled and spoke freely, telling him of the happenings of the day and how much she loved her mistress.

The two were not long in conversation when the double doors swung open, and in stomped Father Wilhelm, ruddy-faced and accompanied by two very tall and austere monks,

"What is this? Doe'st thou neglect thy duties on today of all days. I do hope that you are not in the process of any kind of business, nor any inappropriate deeds in our holiest of places," he spluttered, unaccustomed to even losing his temper.

Barnard was taken aback as the blood drained from his face, "Your Grace, I... I... have nought but the most innocent of intentions. This woman is senior to the household of Lord Wenslau and a kinswoman of our birthplace. I merely..."

"Enough; you will say farewell to this woman and shall promise never to entertain her or anyone who does not represent the business of the church, man or woman!" insisted Wilhelm, quite amazed at his own exertion of authority and with a small lump in his throat.

Barnard was noticeably angry but knew not to challenge Wilhelm's decision, particularly with the monks who were escorting him, former men at arms, loyal to every breath of Wilhelm's and evident by their demeanour.

The junior abbot was now wondering how Father Wilhelm was made aware of his recent activities. Perhaps it was time for him to be more of a friend to his colleagues and associates. His plans were not to be undone after so much preparation and with so much to lose.

Later that evening, Eudda was in deep conversation in the kitchen with Bronwen wearing a very worried expression as Grimbald entered from the stables. Bronwen looked straight at him and shook her head with a look of disappointment. He nodded back, pressing his finger to his lips. "I think we shall partake of supper early this evening. Will you tell my husband, Grimbald?" asked Bronwen.

"He comes not far behind," was the reply.

Wenslau bursted open the door as he did in his awkward manner but more so because his old wound was playing up again, this time quite intensely.

Bronwen begged, "Why do you not have that attended to, husband? There is a good monk in Coverham abbey that everyone has sworn to be of fine knowledge and doctoring."

"I, too, have offered," said Grimbald.

"You should, father. You have had this for two whole years now!" added Inga.

"Maybe I will have you look at my cursed wound, young man. It does not get better with the years." Wenslau's pain was quite evident now, and Bronwen suspected all the riding he had done lately was probably a factor. She urged Grimbald to take a hand and see what he could do.

Grimbald ordered for a bed place to be made up by the fire. He seemed very confident outwardly, but it was quite some time since he last performed anything so invasive. "Lay yourself here, sire, and have your breeks and leggings removed."

Wenslau did as he was told and shakily placed himself on the bed. Bronwen helped him undress. Grimbald was not prepared for the sight of so much damage to the man's groin. A deep scar ran through the inside right of Wenslau's buttock finishing a few inches further up the front of his lower abdomen. Worse still, there was a swollen testicle, or what was left of it, looking very grey and putrid.

"This was done with an axe, sire," said Grimbald.

Wenslau nodded with hesitation, "Aye."

"Close your eyes, sire, and try to relax," ordered Grimbald as he held his hand hovering over the area of the wound, moving slowly like a hawk over its prey. "Two parts of your groin need urgent attention, and another will also if you do not rest after I have tended you. Inga, could you bring my bag with the green leather snake on it? And could you have a half beaker of honey warmed, my lady?" He then took a flask of liquor from his main satchel, mixing it in a second beaker with a dried powder that smelled of mushrooms. "Now drink this, sire," he said.

Within a minute, Wenslau started slurring his words and giggling like a child. Bronwen looked on, quite worried. Inga just giggled along with her father.

"This part will pass, my lady; he will soon be asleep and without pain," he assured.

Sure enough, Wenslau went into a deep sleep, and Grimbald reached into his satchel to retrieve a small, strange-looking blade that had been wrapped in some kind of ointment-impregnated cloth with an awfully pungent smell to it. He then dipped the knife in a potion of wild garlic and peppered water.

Grimbald was starting to feel a tad more confident and asked Aelfswip, Inga, and her mother to look away. Everyone was transfixed and watched in anticipation.

"If I were a common Shaman, I would be asking for the help of the gods at this time, but you can ask for me if you wish," he said with a smile, before plunging the blade into the scarred tissue. There was a sudden oozing of grey and yellowy puss, and the moulding smell of rotted flesh emanated throughout the vicinity. Grimbald told Aelfswip to fetch some clean boiled water to flush out the remaining infection. The remaining operation went well over many hours. The cleaning and tying up of the whole scar tissue was thorough, and meticulously wrapped in a mix of garlic and honey with some finely woven cloth.

Wenslau slept for the rest of the day and through the night, being left to wake when ready. When he did wake, it was with a strangely clear but heavy head. He was very alert to everything around him and smiling to himself for having such clarity of thought. The moment he tried to move, that took the smile off his face. He felt as if being kicked by a horse. The main satisfaction was that the pain was isolated, and he knew he was going to get better. "I cannot thank you enough, my friend. I knew you would fix me," he whispered to Grimbald, who was watching his recovery from a chair by the fire. The softly flickering flames bounced their glow on his face as he smiled.

Grimbald was fairly exhausted himself from the previous day's ordeal and concern over Wenslau. "The war is not over yet. If you rest as you should, sire, I see no reason for you not to be almost as you once were." He was still thinking about what he saw while tending the wound. Visions of what had occurred horrified him, and connections were made that he had not expected. Grimbald realized that the machinations of the abbey were much to do with what many people around were vulnerable to; much of what happened to him was tied to Wenslau's recent history and angst.

Aedric meanwhile did not have to do anything to keep the young warrior occupied for plans to go accordingly.

CHAPTER TWENTY-ONE

The Intricate War

Over recent years, Barnard had become a devastating tactician, not only in his connivances with wealthy landowners and lords but also with his proclivities towards young boys and the novices under his service. His position had afforded him some clemency by a handful of monks in his circle, while others would not dare say anything against him for fear of the consequences. Most of what he achieved was by way of an amazing sense of charm and persuasiveness. Some would say if he wanted to, he could sell Christianity to the devil. In all his dealings, he always had a backup plan and kept himself well guarded by his trusted soldiers, particularly the one who would do most of his dirty work, Hrodgar, a cold, sadistic, expressionless brute. This man was also a tactician and opportunist, one who had gained favour by undertaking all tasks without question.

A meeting took place with Hrodgar, acting on behalf of his master, to finalise the plan to instigate a war among local lords and the gentry. He consulted with a strong ally in the form of Sigeweard, a wealthy and corrupt landowner, vying for chieftainship and power. One of Wenslaus' good friends, Birdos, was to be the first target of their schemes as a trigger to draw out various other factions.

Wenslau had started to move around steadily after a few days, despite warnings from his wife and friends not to expect much of himself. One morning he went outside to take in some air when he came across a group of villagers staring silently up into the woodland behind his house. The light was painfully bright, shining through the gaps in the trees, but he could make out the shape of a man sitting cross-legged, in a praying position, on the middle of a branch. "That could only be the young Grimbald," he said to the audience.

Not long after, a visitor came to the top of the village near Luuah's house, walking alongside a donkey. He wore a mustard-coloured robe with a heavy hood. As the occupants of Luuah's house filed out, he pulled back his hood and looked in their direction with a warm, friendly, and beaming smile; the donkey was looking toward them, also. Fryda came out in her usual threatening manner but, after looking at the stranger, melted in his gaze like others. Luuah was last, fastening up his trousers again after a hearty breakfast. He straight away knew who the man was as they had met on several occasions when they were both out foraging or hunting. Although they had never spoken, there was an understanding. Hilda approached the man and asked what business he might have in the village and with whom.

"He is on his way, young lady; we shall greet when I see him," said the man. Hilda and the others all somehow felt assured by his words. No sooner than he had spoken, Grimbald appeared from behind Wenslau's house and strode up the hill to meet the visitor.

"We look after the donkey, master," offered Luuah.

"I know full well you will," came the reply as the stranger handed over the reins.

Grimbald was enrapt with the presence of his guide and master, who had not aged a day from when they parted all those years ago. Grimbald put out his arms, and they embraced like father and son.

Mochanna pulled back a little and gave one of his wry smiles, saying, "You have been foolish, my boy, so I am here to mend you. And before you ask... I will meet with your friend and host. He is a good man, I know! Before all that, I have a little surprise for you." He blew on an instrument that made a weird echoing hum; some of the stones nearby appeared to move, and all the animals in the village stared in his direction. Everyone close by was astounded as Mochanna said lightly, "A little something I forgot to teach you." A familiar figure came over the brow; Grimbald recognised those vivid red locks. Tears welled in his eyes as he ran to greet Sunni.

"I thank the gods. You are well and unhurt by all that has happened." He immediately realised his last words were somewhat hollow as Sunni smiled with a tinge of sadness, a sadness which he suspected was due partly to her ordeal with the kidnappers. "Come, I will introduce you to my hosts… tis so very good to see you again, Sunni, so very, very good. I must ask you about my sister. I know she is still alive, but I have confusing thoughts as to what is happening to her," added Grimbald, confusing Sunni with his array of thoughts.

"You have changed greatly." She announced.

As the company was about to enter Wenslau's house, Aedric appeared from the stable nearby, dragging a new young boy by the arm. Mochanna could not disguise his immediate loathing for the man and whispered in Grimbald's ear, "Why have you not dispatched this wretch?" quickly rectifying himself with, "Yes, I see, but he has overlived for too long!"

Soon, Wenslau and the guests were around the table, trying to devise a plan to subdue the forthcoming war. Mochanna initiated authority without argument. He insisted no servants be allowed in the house whilst the parlance took place and no one should come in or go out of the village until Wenslau said so. Aedric was extremely angry at being excluded and questioned Bronwen for the logic behind his exclusion, to which Bronwen convincingly replied, "It is for your own safety Aedric and all others of this household."

182

Sunni deferred Grimbald's enquiries of her as the matters to be presently discussed were of more importance. Mochanna had many acquaintances in the region, far more than Grimbald would have ever suspected. The news he shared with his customary advice about who to assassinate was invaluable, even if a tad harsh.

Just as the meeting was about to start, there was a rap at the door… it was Garaint, who did not know if he would be able to attend. "My apologies, one and all. I do not like having to lie of my whereabouts, but as I am an assistant to Godwynn, our healer, I managed to convince his Holiness of your possible need, sire. As explained to me by your maidservant whom I first spoke yesterday."

"Yes, yes, my man, take a seat," ushered Wenslau at the head of the long, creaky table.

Mochanna looked over the monk as if looking over a painting, then immediately turned to Grimbald.

"You have an errand, my lad. One I could not do. You have your guile, and I have mine. I will try to play my part in this skulduggery, but you must lay the path of guilt at someone's feet that cannot be argued against if we are to succeed. So, choose your target wisely, and I recommend you have the three you know are primary offenders executed. Do not try to do this all on your own. Remember the methods I taught you. You have been lazy with your talents. Now prove yourself. You have so much to offer, be the man you can be."

"Where do I come in all of this?" asked Wenslau, feeling weak and rather left out.

"You will have far more to do if you are willing to take my advice, good sir," said Mochanna, knowing exactly how Wenslau would react to a bit of flattery.

"Well, if this young man has as much faith in you as I have in him, I'll swallow my pride with a pail of piss," remarked Wenslau, puffing his chest out and clenching his fist on the table.

The conversation went on for several hours, with several outbursts of surprise by Bronwen, Sunni, Inga, and Wenslau

"You must have your plans in order by tomorrow noon, my boy," ordered Mochanna.

"I think I already have," replied Grimbald rather confidently.

"Look deep, my boy; you cannot afford any slip-up," said Mochanna as he was shown his sleeping place.

The next morning was as bright a day as could ever be. Though slightly chilly, the sun was gently warming the fields. The family was up early. Inga came rushing to her father as he sat uncomfortably in his chair. "The wizard has gone; I thought he was here to help us," she asked.

"You may not see him, Inga, but he will not be far away. Expect him, and he is gone; expect him not, then he appears. He has often said that men are so predictable. We all have our instructions and plans in place," said Grimbald as he came out from the kitchen.

Eudda was instructed to pass on the news to Aedric about the master going to war to settle his loans. Of course, he wanted to know about the master's adversaries and aides. She furnished him with all the knowledge she had on the matter. Aedric, then, asked for permission to go to Coverham as one of his cousins was supposedly there on business and they had not seen each other for *many a year*.

Barnard was in a close meeting with Hrodgar in the abbey garden behind a group of yew trees. He was giving out his instructions when one of his servants came to ask if he could receive the company of Aedric with important news.

"Send him forth," ordered Barnard as Hrodgar, who was about to leave, glanced back at Aedric with complete loathing.

Soon the sound of horses cantering out of the abbey stables could be heard. Aedric, trying to make his voice heard over the rumble of hooves, said, "Father, I do not know if you have set your plans in motion, but I have some strange and interesting news for you."

Barnard grew impatient as Aedric was rather long-winded in explaining things. The monk ordered him to hurry up and tell what was happening. Upon hearing from Aedric, Barnard's face went pale and drawn; his schemes could backfire. He paced up and down for a minute, swearing and cursing, his face was turning red. "You must ride after Hrodgar and tell him to return with his men."

"But Father, I will be missed if I am gone too long, and I fear that Hrodgar does not take too kindly to me," protested Aedric.

"You have been well rewarded in the past, my man. Take heed if you know what is good for you. You will do as I say. Hrodgar must not meet with Sigeweard of Hawick; I have had my suspicions of that man all along. His wealth came too quickly. Hrodgar must return at the earliest," Barnard replied through gritted teeth.

"Who shall I take with me, Father?" asked Aedric.

"No one, you must go alone with the utmost secrecy! Leave now, or we may be too late," the monk commanded.

A very worried Aedric was duly provided a fast and sturdy horse; he nervously mounted him. The horse started to move as he was mounting, making him more anxious.

Just outside the gates facing west were three figures standing by their horses. As soon as Aedric left the abbey, one of the onlookers mounted and rode steadily in the same direction.

Barnard was angered by the turn of events and, for once, did not know who he could truly trust. He had a meeting with Father Wilhelm and felt quite uneasy about the matter apart from the inconvenience to his plans. Lylleborne was a good half-day's ride from Coverham, and Aedric was apprehensive of being kicked out of his job before managing to accrue enough wealth to leave Wenslau's service. Dark clouds were sweeping over the valley, and there were wolves and wild boars to worry about as a loan traveller. He suddenly remembered a shortcut across the fields that might help him to catch up with Hrodgar. The wind picked up, making things worse as the horse became a little skittish. Aedric was about to make a turn in a small copse, a shrill gurgling sound emitted from the trees. The horse reared up and threw him onto the rough ground. Suddenly from nowhere, came a pungent-smelling piece of rag cloth, smacking him in the face. As he tried to throw away the rag, Aedric noticed runic symbols on it that signified only one thing.

In the near distance, Hrodgar and his men were halted by a sickening, blood-curdling scream and the sound of a hungry pack of wolves. He said in his usual callous way, "Whoever that was, they are no more, and we have less to worry about as the wolves are fed." One of his loyal men sniggered and nodded whilst the others cringed. Shortly after... the horse Aedric was riding galloped straight past the soldiers, fuelled with dire terror. "Go and catch him," ordered Hrodgar to two of his men, half recognising the steed. The two men raced after the wild stallion until they were both out of sight. Hrodgar's remaining five men argued about what had happened earlier and made jokes about their comrades chasing after the frightened horse. A little while later, as the troupe neared a rise, they could see three horses tied together, standing still as if hypnotised to the spot.

Hrodgar was not a man to be easily unsettled, but events were turning out to be unlike anything he had known before. He ordered the men to dismount and circle around the area where the tethered horses were. The men scoured every inch of the site, but there was no sign of even the slightest scuffle. Hrodgar slowly made his way to the three horses and looked at them for cuts, marks, or loss of some of their saddlery. They were clean and extremely calm. He summoned his men and carried on with their journey. The road was starting to get busy with traffic from the town to nearby villages. One wagon driven by an old, hooded figure passed the men, going back towards Coverham with several dead bodies piled up on top of one another. It would not be unusual for people to be sent to for burial, but Hrodgar was feeling disturbed. He turned in his saddle, considering whether or not to take a look but decided it would be wiser to leave them alone in case of any pestilence as there was a recent outbreak in the area. "Master, do you want me to have a look?" asked one of his men, who also turned in his saddle.

"No, we have work to do, an army to organise; we carry ourselves on. Let there be no more distractions," he declared angrily.

As the troupe was riding into Lylleborne, one of the soldiers spotted a long line of armed men slowly marching away from the town on the western road. "What goes there?" he shouted, pointing to the line and looking at Hrodgar.

The men hurried into the town; Hrodgar was getting frustrated with the confusing and inexplicable events. Everyone dismounted as they neared the long hall; the streets were clean and tidy, everything orderly, even the houses that looked upon the hall in their neat rows. The people of the town had a sense of presence and liked to dress well, even when working. Sigeweard expected his people to do well and show it through their actions.

Four heavily armed guards came to meet Hrodgar and his men, one of whom he knew straight away as he, too, had served in the church some years ago. Hrodgar looked at him up and down disapprovingly without saying a word. He ordered his men to wait behind and went ahead.

The main chamber of the hall was elegantly decorated, bustling with monks and people busy with their daily business routines, and quite noisy. Sigeweard was consulting with two lords and referring them to a selection of papers.

Hrodgar impatiently burst out a question, "Sir, I need to know what has become of our arrangement; time is of the essence?"

Sigeweard turned to look at Hrodgar with obvious anger at his interruption and blasted, "You should communicate more efficiently with your master. The monks left some time ago. My services, including those of my friends here, are no longer required. Father Steven said you had chosen another course of action. It is of no matter as we were intended to meet this very week. So be on your way and tell your master to no longer seek my services… or my friends, for such time wasting."

"Father Steven?" queried Hrodgar. "I know of no Father Steven; there must be some mistake."

"Not on my part, soldier, not on my part," stated Sigeweard as the two Lords looked at Hrodgar disparagingly. "There was a small party of them. They left about an hour or so back; you may question them if you find them."

Hrodgar gathered his men and rode urgently after being directed the way the monks had left.

CHAPTER TWENTY-TWO

Fair Play

Wenslau had made a special effort to ride his horse into Coverham with a small but sufficient army to wipe out the garrison at the abbey. Grimbald had urged him to make the journey in person and to take Esmond and Eudda with him while he and Luuah led a bigger unit to the east. "We shall meet at dusk, should all go to plan," said Grimbald as he and the army rode away.

Not long after passing Hrodgar and his men, the old man, with the cartload of bodies, got off his cart and went to retrieve the body of Aedric; his throat torn out, but the body fully intact. The man just muttered to himself, "At last, dispatched!" As he pulled back his hood, Mochanna declared rather factually, "Your wolves are no match for mine." Talking to a standing form by the body, its face appeared sorrowful and forlorn as it slowly dispersed into the air. As he drove the wagon nearer to Coverham, Mochanna spotted a young lad by the roadside who looked like an escaped slave, sleeping rough and wild. "BOY," he shouted and then said, "NO... do not run away. I am about to give you a new life and some money!"

The boy thought the man must be mad and was even more frightened when he saw the bodies. He picked up a nearby stick that could probably do a great deal of damage, he thought. "I am not afraid," he declared with a tremor in his voice. "Leave me be, old man," he shouted as he stumbled at the edge of a dyke.

Mochanna wiped the mud and wax off his face that made him look old, pulled out a purse and threw it at the boy, then stood with his hands on his hips, waiting for a response.

"Is this truly for me? You do not want to bugger me, are you? I have had enough of that. It is why I am running away," said the boy with a certain desperation in his voice.

"Be assured, lad, my last desire does not include a boy's buttocks. I need you to fulfil an urgent mission. If you do exactly as I ask and say exactly what I tell you, you will be able to start a new life. For one thing, you will have a cart from which to do business. How many boys of fourteen winters can say that?" Mochanna said with a wry smile.

"You mean the cart will be mine when I have done your errand," said the young man, quite astonished.

"It already is, my boy, if you should look closely at the axle," Mochanna replied.

The boy looked down cautiously at the axle and back at Mochanna suspiciously. There on the axle was his name written in runic script.

"What does it say?" asked the boy.

"It spells out your name in Runes, my lad, and it would pay you to learn them. Edgar, is it not?"

Edgar was dumbfounded, but he had started to realise this man was a wizard and no ordinary one. *It must be that ghostly wizard, the one who people says does funny tricks and healings, who keeps disappearing,* he thought.

Mochanna gave his instructions to the lad and said, "You know how to drive a cart, do you not?" and disappeared before the boy could answer. Edgar looked around whilst staying on the seat of the wagon for a short time, then drove off as per instructions. The cob was very responsive and good-natured, he seemed to fit the name Edgar like his new master, so his full name became Edgar Also or just Ed for travelling orders. Edgar was genuinely excited at what he had acquired but wondered what kind of a bargain he'd let himself in. As promised, he did not look upon his cargo until he had arrived in Coverham Abbey. Nearly a mile before his destination, Edgar came upon a young woman with wild red hair waving him down to ask for a lift into the abbey. "If you do not mind the bodies, climb up," he said.

"Nay, I have seen much death in recent times, young lad. This will not bother me as much as my sore feet," she stated.

As the wagon neared Coverham, there was much activity; many armed men roamed the streets of the abbey town. Sitting on a large grey steed outside the front of the abbey was Wenslau, asking nervous abbey soldiers for an audience with the abbot. After a few minutes, Barnard made an appearance and asked in his smooth-tongued manner, "What is this extraordinary visit all about, sir? We are most honoured for you to call. Can I be of help?"

"I think you would help if you brought out your master, my man. I am here on urgent business…"

Suddenly a side door flew open, and the abbot with a few more soldiers, monks, and novices, scurried into the side yard.

The abbot, also somewhat nervous, asked Wenslau if he would care to come to chambers for a discussion and tried to usher everyone away, including Barnard.

Barnard was not going to be dismissed so easily, as he was growing very suspicious of what might be occurring. He tried to make his objections known, insisting on a more visible meeting. The abbot would not give in.

"No, I will not come in, but I will talk with you on neutral ground. There, the blacksmiths, that will do," Wenslau insisted and told the blacksmith to make way. Wenslau and the abbot were making their way to the blacksmiths when a strong wind blew up the covers of the bodies on the wagon, revealing one dead Aedric on the very top with some of Barnard's best scouts. Many surprised souls, with their mouths open, witnessed the sight. Wenslau had expected the outcome but not as public and open as this.

"This is your man, is it not?" said Barnard to Wenslau at some distance.

"I am not sure if he was mine," replied Wenslau cryptically, looking Barnard straight in the eye.

"You knew him, Father Barnard." said the abbot, "I have seen you in his company several times."

Wenslau turned to look at the abbot, who said quietly, "I think I now know some of what this may be about."

The two moved closer to the blacksmith's brazier as it started to snow. They talked for over an hour as if they had known each other since childhood, laughing occasionally and then with odd outbursts of "What" or "Eh?"

Everyone in the vicinity was freezing; Wenslau's men decided to ride up and down to keep themselves warm while most of the monks went inside.

There were just Barnard and a couple of his loyal followers. He went over to the cart to see what had happened to Aedric, asking the boy who he was and how he came to have the bodies. Sunni, who had been given a lift and sat beside him, said, "You ask a lot for a monk?"

Barnard was aware he was being watched and replied cautiously, "I am merely curious and concerned. There is nothing dubious to the matters of their eventual interment."

Sunni smiled a knowing smile before Edgar told Barnard everything he was instructed to. Barnard was dubious about the cause of their death and was curious why their bodies were sent back to Coverham Abbey. He, however, decided to be extra cautious as many of Wenslau's men were listening in.

Approximately fifteen miles away to the north of Wenslau's leigh, Mochanna, Garaint, and a group of men dressed as monks were changing their clothes to ready themselves for a battle. They were about to meet up with Grimbald and his forces, but before that, coming close behind them were Hrodgar and his men. As they started to pass Mochanna and company, Hrodgar, being somewhat suspicious of the group, asked if they had seen a party of monks going this way and suddenly recognised Garaint.

"What are you doing among these men?" asked Hrodgar angrily.

Instantly one of Hrodgar's men saw the robes half tucked away that the rest of the men had disguised themselves in, yelling, "See here!"

Hrodgar and his men all drew their swords. Out of nowhere, there was an eerie noise that spooked their horses. Three of the riders, including Hrodgar, were thrown to the ground. One surprising thing that became evident was that Hrodgar showed no pain because, being one of life's oddities, he could not feel it. Mochanna knew there was something strange about him apart from his demeanour but did not suspect this.

The two mounted men were soon pulled off as they swayed around and fought with Mochanna's soldiers. Even Garaint prepared himself for battle with a fine sword of his own. Hrodgar steadied himself and headed straight for Mochanna, who stared at the warrior. Hrodgar was not used to men being unafraid of him, which made him even angrier. Two men tried to intervene but were gravely wounded trying to defend the wizard. Hrodgar challenged Mochanna to arm himself and fight him, clashing his shield and sword together.

"You have all the weapons I need!" replied Mochanna sarcastically but with a little trepidation. This was a man who felt no pain, so he would have to act swiftly. His moment came as the knight lunged forward. Mochanna quickly grabbed Hrodgar's sword arm, spinning himself backwards into the knight's face with the back of his head and using the axis of Hrodgar's shield arm to throw himself behind Hrodgar. As the knight was dazed, Mochanna pulled out his seaxa and cut the hamstrings. The knight fell to the floor on his knees whereupon Mochanna grabbed his head and speedily sliced open his neck. The knight's face said everything that a man who thought he was invincible could say. As the blood gushed its way down his armoured tunic, he spluttered into the chasm–his final journey.

Hrodgar's remaining men, seeing what happened, threw down their weapons and yielded. Mochanna ordered everyone to carry on without him; he would see to the prisoners and meet them later. The men who were with him obeyed his command respectfully. Garaint could not believe the stealth and presence of this man, not knowing whether to count him as a demon or a friend. For the time being, he would give the wizard the benefit of the doubt. Mochanna led the tethered prisoners by horse on a shortcut back to Coverham. Some of the soldiers left with Garaint wondered if those prisoners would ever really see Coverham Abbey again.

Back at the abbey, Barnard was getting anxious as his plans were starting to fall apart. He thought Sigeweard had Wenslau in his pocket and decided it would be better to leave well alone rather than lose good men in battle. All he had to rely on now was his other ally Wealdmaer, but Barnard was unsure of the size and strength of Wenslau's army. He seemed to have a huge following. The monk would have to make some possible escape plan should all go wrong.

The only thing that drove Wealdmaer was the possibility of inheriting a plethora of lands and itinerant villages. He had no head for the politics of the church nor real loyalty to Barnard.

The weather had become intolerable as the snow bit into the faces of Wenslau's army on their journey to a berewick just south of Thresca.

Wealdmaer had been summoned earlier that day to the Great Hall at Thresca to meet with King Aldfrith by a troupe of his finest soldiers, made evident by their fine tunics and armoury. The matter had not been disclosed, but he would not dare decline the invitation. Aldfrith took no prisoners when it came to matters of court. Like many kings of his time, rule by fear and intimidation was the order of the day.

Wealdmaer duly arrived at the Great Hall in Thresca. It was more like a village than a town, but it hosted many an important event, subsidiary to the Halls of Inhrypum, the home of Great Halls of Justice and Christian learning north of Eorforwic. He had brought over two hundred men with him, having been told that he may be needed in battle by a trusted source. As Wealdmaer walked through the entrance hall, he saw two of Barnard's cohort monks standing by the king, looking rather worried. Unsure how to prepare himself, he ordered his four bodyguards to stay back in case they should be questioned. Unbeknown to him, Wealdmaer's son Ealdred had come to Thresca to the aid of his father, and waited outside for him to return.

The meeting with Wealdmaer did not go well, as Aldfrith's plans were thwarted by the interventions of Barnard and all his associates. Aldfrith had captured and tortured one of Barnard's loyal monks into revealing his master's name and what he knew of his plans. Unfortunately, one of the tortured monks' cohorts managed to escape and get back to warn Barnard of possible reprisals.

Several miles back, Wenslau and his men took shelter in the nearby forest awaiting news of the meeting between Wealdmaer and King Aldfrith. It wasn't long before two of Wenslau's men, accompanied by three of Aldfrith's guards, came with word of events and what must now take place. Not far behind came Grimbald with seventeen mighty warriors in his company.

"Hail, sire, I have brought a few of my friends and soldiers of Lord Coenedd. They are a small army of men, great in their accomplishments. Lord Coenedd pays his respects and wishes you well in your battle... our battle," said Grimbald with conviction.

The weather improved slightly as the sun started to shine through, the wind easing, and a soft flutter of snow gently falling as pale blue skies started to nudge between the clouds. Loki gave a loud bark in the relative stillness of the men sheltering in the forest. Grimbald knew that bark and what it meant.

"We must ready ourselves to that field yonder," ushered Grimbald, pointing southwest of Thresca. "The time is near and a battle to be won," he added nervously.

Wealdmaer was now on an errand of his own making but nothing as he had planned. Siegaweard's men were supposed to be at his disposal to ensure victory, but they had not arrived. Aldfrith was not supposed to be aware of this feud, nor was he expected to be in this part of the country, and worst of all, Wealdmaer's son was now being held captive as a guarantee that the battle would be *a fair play*. Aldfrith's wife, Cuthburh, had little part to play in that decision.

One of Wealdmaer's men suggested riding back to Maessaham for more troupes, but he was fearful of the consequences to his son's life. The best he could hope for was that word would pass around to those loyal and indebted to him to come to his aid. All his hopes and wishes were to be addressed on the battlefield. Wenslau's men gradually made their way out of the forest. Grimbald stood off to one side with his entourage and quietly mouthed the words behind his hand to Wenslau, "Are you able, sire."

Wenslau nodded assuredly, then spoke to his men about their plan of attack, "I know this fox. He will sacrifice his foot soldiers to make a break through our line. Therefore, we shall not give him a line. Archers, I want you to take down the riders of his left and right flanks so that he has to make a line. I want my foot soldiers at the rear so that when we break their rank, you will come between with your pikes and retreat when you have taken your toll, ready to come forth again..."

Grimbald was mightily impressed with Wenslau and could understand why he rose to his position. The respect and honour he showed were equally rewarded. Every man was ready and willing to do their duty. Much to Grimbald's horror, a group of Wealdmaer's men turned out to be the same men who were his captors some weeks earlier. They recognised him but showed complete contempt, spitting in his direction and bandying their weapons in the air. As the feud commenced, Grimbald rode a distance away, feigning injury. Some of his friends kept a close eye in case anything untoward should happen. Wealdmaer shouted for the filthy four to follow and help him; only one of the four did as requested while the other three surrounded Grimbald. He raised his hand and made an eerie noise; all three horses rose up and threw their riders. As one man was falling, Grimbald sliced off his sword arm and gashed his eyes. The second man had a spear that Grimbald grabbed quickly and swiftly beheaded him before he could react. The third fighting man, who spat in his direction, offered Grimbald a fair fight, to which Grimbald replied, "How could you know of such." The man sneakily tried to draw a large knife from behind his back, and just as he started to push it forward, Grimbald stuck his sword in the inside edge of the man's forearm rendering him incapable of gripping his sword. As the sword dropped to the floor, Grimbald took off the man's knife arm up to the elbow. "That is a debt paid," he stated.

The man went crazy with rage, tears burst out of his eyes and slavered the words, "Aye, but your other friend was dogmeat for the best part." He tried to laugh, but the pain was intense.

Grimbald lost his temper more than he ever thought he could and produced a wire-reinforced whip. He laid into the crazy figure with such frenzy that within seconds, the man was flayed alive and unrecognisable. He didn't remain alive for long as the blood quickly drained into the field. No sooner had he done the deed, Grimbald loathed himself for such actions, even if this man was so evil. The fourth member of the unsavoury group would later be found dead on the battlefield, accidentally speared in the neck by one of Wealdmaer's own foot soldiers as he tried to retreat.

The battle was bloody, and Wenslau felt almost ashamed that after nearly two hours, it was won too easily with very few casualties of his own. Wealdmaer's men were cruelly beaten, and he was fatally wounded in the chest by one of

Grimbald's friends. Four horsemen arrived soon after the battle, Aldfrith's personal guards. They invited Wenslau and some of his close allies to meet with him at Thresca if he felt able, of course.

CHAPTER TWENTY-THREE

A Just Man

Wenslau and seven of his best men, including Grimbald, slowly ambled into Thresca, their horses still panting and sweating from the battle. Many people in the streets who were his supporters cheered after their years of suppression and heavy taxes by Wealdmaer. They knew of this Reeve to be a noble and fair.

Wenslau and company were guided to the entrance of the great hall. Once escorted inside, they saw Wealdmaer's son, Ealdred, standing between two giants of men with finely platted blonde hair. Aldfrith waved the tired party forward and ordered for the table on the south wall to be filled with food, ale, and wine. There were many furnishings and accoutrements the royal couple had brought with them to show off their wealth. The walls held many shields and weapons of vanquished foes, including their joint family's regalia. The golden and silver glints were frequently rippling their lustre to the walls by the glow of the basket fires placed around the hall.

"Be seated; we will join you anon." said the king. The company all grouped, eyes wide open to the beautiful food and accompaniments laid before them. Bowls of warm water and scented oils were on a separate table for them to wash before dining with soft linen towels. Aldfrith and his wife Cuthburh would be seated at either end of the long table. Wenslau was seated next to Aldfrith, who patted him on the shoulder as he took his place, smiling at a man who looked his age.

"Well fought, bold Wenslau," the queen congratulated. "so, to all of you!" as she raised a goblet.

In a noticeably short time, Ealdred grew angry, upset, and screamed, "What of my father, lord?" The guards hurriedly kicked his shins away and placed him kneeling on the floor with his head bowed, by which time he was sobbing. He was a young man of sensitivities, not really a leader of his time. Wenslau looked at him pitifully, saying to the guards, "It would please me if you would let him stand. I do not want the son to pay for the misdeeds of the father."

The guards looked to their king, who acceded to the request with a simple nod.

"My good Lord, this young man may want your throat one day," whispered the king to Wenslau.

"I do hope not, sire. I would rather become peaceful neighbours, at the least," Wenslau whispered in return.

The king pulled his head back in surprise, "But this boy is the only heir; you would be well within your rights to take his lands and property after what his father had tried to do to you. You could banish the boy if needs be."

Wenslau was not surprised by the severe tones of Aldfrith; it was normal for most kings to act in such a way. He wondered if Aldfrith wanted to take the properties for himself, but Aldfrith added. "Whatever you decide, I shall oversee these lands for some time to come for a small revenue, as you know. So, if you wish the lad..."

Grimbald sitting opposite, quietly interrupted, slightly annoying Aldfrith. "Forgive me, sire, but is it not wiser for my good friend to allot himself some spoils so as not to give the impression of being guilty and weak spirit," he started to whisper, "Better still, he shows modest compassion by putting young Ealdred to contractual obligations. As the boy follows Christian traditions, this should be of some acceptance concerning his position for the time being. And your armies would assuredly be of greater number in this agreement, sire."

Aldfrith clenched his finely platted beard and asked Wenslau who his impetuous friend was. Wenslau generously identified him, "He is as close a friend as any man could have, and I have some very close friends here indeed." All of Wenslau's men understood without envy how much Grimbald had done for him in the short time they had known each other, including many of the village folk.

"Is it perhaps that you are an opportunist young knight, vying for a position of your own? Do you seek some reward for the deeds thus far?" asked the King.

"Sire, my reward is the friendship of all men, women, and their kindred. These things I have been taught by an incredibly wise man, not Christian and certainly no ordinary man in any sense of the word. I seek not possessions, for as we know, they can be the aim of those who do not have, those of a jealous mind, the thief, or the trickster. Perhaps what I aspire to the most is family... which I have lost." Grimbald suddenly paused, staring at the wall, thinking of his sister, and remembered some of Mochanna's words.

Queen Cuthburh was fascinated with Grimbald and begged him to tell them more of his deeds, ventures, and beliefs.

At first, he tried to avoid talking about himself for fear of boring everyone. They all sat and listened to Grimbald's diluted version of events that were no less fascinating. How his family was slaughtered, and how he was taken in and trained by Mochanna. He told of his year fishing with Danish fishermen, later joining up with a Jute tribe and being adopted as one of their kind and soon becoming a mercenary for whoever needed him. During this saga of events, Wenslau excused himself to go and talk to Ealdred to give him some comfort, hopefully. Aldfrith offered for the young man to join his father in another chamber where he lay dying; Wenslau insisted on going with him.

Wenslau had Ealdred released from the auspices of the guards and insisted on walking together, but also that he should listen for a moment before seeing his father. The two stood outside the door for quite some time. Ealdred nodded toward the end of their conversation but begged to see his father alone, to which Wenslau agreed.

In the field where the battle took place, the wounded and beaten were transported back home in carts and conveyance. Wenslau had agreed that of all those whose horses were still able, to keep them and return in peace. Some of Lord Coenedd's soldiers were asked to oversee the return of the defeated men and a few fighting women. Those lying dead would be collected over a matter of days and, if not claimed within the week, would be buried in unconsecrated ground at the local church. Customarily the victor would compensate the landowner from his spoils, but Aldfrith had stepped in to honour his friend.

The celebrations and festivities went well, with a tinge of sadness for Wenslau, Grimbald, and a couple of others. They were all provided with first-class accommodation, having servants to bathe them and see to their every need. Before wishing everyone a good night's sleep, Aldfrith declared to Wenslau, "You have one more duty to perform in the morning, my friend. In the meantime, I wish you an exceptionally good night's sleep, all of you. The servants will wake you at the due hour." Wenslau was too exhausted to question his meaning.

Cuthburh echoed the same sentiment and gently grabbed Grimbald's arm with an endearing smile that worried him, "Good night, young sir," she uttered. Aldfrith could see she had a twinkle in her eye for him, and it wasn't the first time. As Grimbald looked toward the king, Aldfrith just winked at him knowingly and immediately put his mind at rest.

Wenslau slept peacefully for the first few hours but so much went on in his mind after going to the toilet. His responsibilities to another territory, not entirely his, what kind of contract to draw up to keep the peace, missing his own hearth and chuntering wife and daughter. And now he still has another duty to perform for his greatest ally, "what on earth could it be?" Slowly he drifted back to sleep again.

Suddenly Wenslau awoke with a start; there was a lot of activity, and one of the servants, a young boy looking very frightened, came into his chamber, "Sire, I have been told to shout, to wake you, this is the fourth time, and I may be in a great pot of trouble. Could you please arise and be ready for his majesty? I can help if you wish."

"Sheiss, nay, your duty's done, boy. I will be about presently, convey my apologies. Here." He threw the boy a penninga which he sharply picked up and polished on his leggings.

Loki wondered into his room as if to usher him out. Then the giant twins came to escort him through to the main hall, where everyone stood regimentally by the columns down the hall. Aldfrith and Cuthburh were seated on their thrones, and a priest was standing beside them.

Wenslau muttered, "By the gods, sire, I must apologise. Are we expecting somebody of importance?"

"You could say that," replied the king, to which everyone in the hall burst out laughing, many with tears in their eyes at Wenslau's expression.

Wenslau looked around and saw Rowe, who pointed with an open hand at the front of the hall, saying, "For you!"

Before him was a tabard and shield, with Wenslau's family emblems emboldened upon them, held by two servants in attendance. From the back of the hall came the sound of trumpets to initiate proceedings. Wenslau took his place while still looking around, quite stunned, and duly wore the shield and tabard as instructed.

Aldfrith and Cuthburh smiled down fondly as the trumpeter played out his tune. The king announced to all in attendance how he was about to officially knight Wenslau for his services to the king and country, a long overdue debt to a loyal and worthy servant. In total, the service lasted about an hour due to the introduction of church rules and regulations for such a ceremony. At the penultimate point, Aldfrith asked Wenslau to give up his sword, causing him to look somewhat confused again. Aldfrith smiled and held out a brand-new sword saying, "Here I give you one of the finest swords ever to be made. Oswin, my very own personal smith, one of the Belgae, hath only yesterday, finished the fashioning of it. You must give it a worthy name, Lord Wenslau."

Wenslau was ecstatic to have such a beautiful addition to his armoury, knowing the reputation of the Belgae metalsmiths, and thought, *I must only ever use this if in battle at the king's side.* Grimbald knew straight away how he would feel about this gift, as did Rowe and Haydn.

The newly appointed knight was eager to gather his men together and get home, but Aldfrith insisted Wenslau do one more thing. As he had the deputy abbot of Inhrypum at his disposal, the contractual arrangements could be drawn up between him and Ealdred. Wenslau was overly generous during the making of the contract and would have to be reminded of his position and how people might try to take advantage of his nature. He kept insisting in his fit of temper that if anyone tried to take him for a fool, he would have their heads. This everyone knew, but Aldfrith pointed out it should not come to that, and he should take the time to prepare carefully in the first place. As instructed, so he did. It was quite evident at the outset that His Lordship was a bad reader and hardly knew any Latin.

Ealdred was an educated young man and cautiously scrutinised the terms of the contract. He was mostly satisfied with the terms but, like Wenslau, was in a hurry to get back home to bury his father. Ealdred was ashamed that his father's greed had brought on his own demise with all the years of scheming with the deviant monk from Coverham. *Barnard had visited far too often for it to be a church business,* he thought. "Maybe this was a new beginning?"

By midday, everyone was on their way home. Wenslau insisted that Ealdred ride with him until they reached Meassaham.

Ealdred advised Wenslau that his mother Etheldreda, was a very venomous creature when scorned or cornered and that she may try to stir up trouble, regardless of what Wealdmaer had done.

Wenslau assured Ealdred that he had dealt with this kind of situation before and would deal with her alone in a quiet corner.

The wind was blowing intermittently and fairly strongly from the east; the temperature kept rising and falling as they neared Meassaham.

Ealdred spotted his mother with a small group of soldiers coming towards them. She was angry and tearful at the same time, saying, "Thank god you were spared, my dearest boy." Then she turned her wet face toward Wenslau, glowering.   Grimbald was further back, curious as to how his friend was going to handle this situation.

As Wenslau and a few of his close companions dismounted, including Grimbald. Ealdred declared. "Mother, we have lost a battle, our father, and could have lost all our lands and more to Lord Wenslau. He has shown favour and mercy in binding us to a contract that is more than fair and just. I know you grieve, are angry, and are very sad, but we have another chance. Please do not be foolish in your grief; we have suffered enough."

As if she had not heard what her son had said, Etheldreda stood squarely up to Wenslau, looked him straight in the eye, and spat in his face. Wenslau immediately spat back in her face, punched her in the jaw, and knocked her out.

Ealdred looked on, extremely worried, as Wenslau had her taken unconscious to a nearby house where they were to be left alone until he had put her to rights. Grimbald came up alongside the young man and comforted him with the fact that Wenslau intended no more harm on his mother but that she would be made to see the folly of her vengeful spirit.

All was quiet in the house for some time, then suddenly Etheldreda screamed in protest with a resounding "NO-O-O." Wenslau never raised his voice once, and within an hour, all was over. Etheldreda came out first, looking pale, demure, and ghostly. Wenslau followed with his hand resting on the hilt of his new sword and nodded at Grimbald with that just-as-you-thought-I-would look.

Ealdred tried to speak to his mother, but she was silent, not looking up as Wenslau and the party left for home.

Bronwen and some of her friends were taking a sauna in the middle of the village when, without any hesitation, in walked Mochanna and, matter of factly, announced that Wenslau would be here within the next hour, then just walked out again. All the women looked a little bit startled but unphased and decided to terminate their pleasures to greet their husbands and loved ones. "He is a strange one, that sorcerer. He has only one light in his head, and that's for a lone space," declared one of the women. As all the women stepped outside, Bronwen called to Eich, "Did you know of his master's return, Eich?"

"Aye, the spirit of the sky... him there, told me, so it must be right!" the blacksmith responded sarcastically, pointing at Mochanna striding to the top of the village with his donkey following behind and staff waving in the air as he told the rest of the village.

Mochanna did not often get animated about anything, but he felt a sense of pride in forming the union of people at the outset of recent events and the satisfactory result for all concerned. All, that is, bar one.

Soon the slow ambling party of warriors appeared at the brow of the village. Bronwen could not hide her glee at seeing her husband home and unscathed for once.

"I am now the official lord of this village and these lands. I have inherited as guardian incumbent the estates of the deceased Lord Wealdmaer," stated Wenslau, raising his new sword and shield. The whole village cheered, and the word quickly spread far and wide. This was a great day for Wenslau's dale and his people.

Wenslau eased himself out of his saddle, feeling rather stiff from his still weakened groin and all the riding. Everyone took their lead from him and dismounted, ready to meet their kinfolk. Just as Grimbald was dismounting, Mochanna walked up to him and said, "Welcome back, Alfvén."

Grimbald did not know what to say; he had not heard that name for nearly two years. He simply looked at the wizard questioningly. Mochanna being as cryptic as he liked to be, just twisted his head with a cheeky grin. Composing himself, Grimbald enquired about Mochanna's own undertakings, to which he replied, "I am not yet finished, my boy. There is a demon making strides for Eorforwic with stolen treasures. I have made it my personal promise to afford him some discomfort and put some things to rights."

"Shall I ride with you, master?" Grimbald asked.

Mochanna announced, "Alas, that cannot be allowed, young man. You are not ready. You still have much to learn, and you must heed some of the warnings that will come your way in many guises. Do not let go of your instincts; keep them tuned and tested constantly. I must go now and do not know if or when we will meet again, but you will know when I am near. Farewell, young knight and wizard, stay at your wits." He turned away from Grimbald as if he hadn't cared, went up to Wenslau, grabbed him by the arm, and said, "There will always be warmth in these lands that you have made for people to wander through. Though much will change over the years, your legacy will last a very long time. Farewell, friend. Stay as you are." Everyone in the vicinity called his name, some shouting farewell wizard, but he never looked back once. He just waved his staff in the air, and his donkey trotted up behind him.

CHAPTER TWENTY-FOUR

The Harsh Justice

Several months later, many territorial issues were settled with the help of Grimbald and the intervention of Abbot Wilhelm, who made himself available now that the malevolent Barnard was no longer around. In fact, the abbot brought about a much greater sense of order in everyone's lives and thoroughly enjoyed doing so.

The season was trying to bring the spring weather but for a few too many days of icy rain. So, most of the folk were engaged in repairing walls, fences, enclosures, and styes. Women and children were checking grain for seed from last year while most of the slaves were clearing the fields of weeds and rocks, the weeds for compost and the rocks stored for foundation ballast; everything was used.

Grimbald would always go out and help whoever needed it, as well as tending to the sick. Sunni often worked alongside him; they shared a great bond. She was learning to be a medicine woman but was also seeking the help of a monk at Coverham, who Wilhelm had allowed as a special favour to Wenslau. Grimbald and Sunni would often comfort each other as and when they felt either he went to her bed or she went to his.

As Sunnandaeg mornings were becoming more Christianised, most people were observing the faith, many still with a foot in each camp. One particular Sunnandaeg Grimbald and Sunni lay together and were talking about their aims and what they wished to do. Grimbald suddenly stopped at one point and could not continue; he felt a lump in his throat as if he were going to be unable to swallow. "This is the sign, Mochanna told me about," exclaimed Sunni as she passed him some water from a bowl. "What do you mean?" he asked.

Sunni continued, "He asked me not to tell you what I know until you have made good here with Wenslau and his people, which included me and what you have taught me."

Grimbald looked at her, waiting for the next part of her confession. "When I came to the village with him, I wanted to tell you there and then. It concerns Agatha…" (He started to get agitated, glaring at her) "I saw her briefly, at least, I think it was her. Her hair was not so light, but she had the right features. She was upon a cart heading toward south Deira. I was going to shout, but a man grabbed me from behind and was about to hit me, thinking

I was someone else. It all happened quickly at a little market town called Picheringa, where Mochanna had arranged to meet me. She looked incredibly sad but healthy enough. She was with a family, and since she was riding up front, perhaps she was not a slave. I made enquiries but could not make sense of anything I was told?"

"What do you mean?" asked Grimbald.

"Well, the people I first asked were at a trinket stall, and they said she was choosing items for the family but not looking at them like anyone would. She just touched them and said yay or nay. The stallholders thought she was a witch. When I asked if they had heard her name, they merely said, girl. I also asked at another stall where she had been, but it was much the same. But they did hear them say about going to Oolesby near the coast, in Lindsey. Maybe there is family in those parts?"

"You said all this, and yet I know there is something more," said Grimbald.

"By the gods, he did teach you well. Yes, it was the very day he was leaving the village on that small path east of the woods. I saw him talking to some small people with what looked like large heads. I couldn't see their faces; they both wore hoods. At first, I thought they were children, but they moved in such a way, that was with authority, and most strange of all, there was no sound coming from anyone, as if they were all behind some kind of wall or whispering. Mochanna saw me and put his hand out for me to stay where I stood. As he approached me, the figures disappeared, and I heard an eerie humming noise in the woods where a blinding bright light suddenly flashed. I was about to ask Mochanna who and what had happened when the thought was pushed out of my mind as soon as he looked me in the eye and put his hand on my shoulder."

Grimbald mused, "The sly old dog. He knew I would not have lingered, knowing she was near. I am wondering if he bewitched me by being unable to sense her presence. She is the only one I have had difficulty seeing in my mind's eye. There was always a shifting feeling like a strong tide whenever I tried to seek her. Oddly enough, I believe the spell has broken because I am now seeing her very clearly. I will be away tomorrow. Will you come with me?"

"I wondered when this day would come, what I would do? We are good together... but I feel a sense of belonging for the first time since I was a child. This village, the people, Lord Wenslau and Lady Bronwen, who I have a great liking for. I believe this is where I wish to stay. I would be happy to work for anyone here to earn my keep. You must say farewell to everybody, and perhaps one day, you will come back to us. I will miss you greatly," sighed Sunni. "When you find Agatha... be careful how you treat her, Grim; she may have been badly used?"

He nodded pensively.

The rest of the day, Grimbald made his way around the village, saying his farewells, also seeing that his horse, Aylmer, was well examined and treated by Eich. Aylmer was almost fully recovered, but Grimbald remembers him being skittish at the battle when he took on the three men from Esingtun. There was a history to be uncovered in that place for the sake of his former friends, but for now, he wished to find his sister.

The morning came, and Sunni said goodbye from the lodge they had been staying in, kissing him heartily on the lips and telling him to take a lucky clover she had pressed in between two slivers of wood tied with twine.

As he ventured outside, there was a small gathering of people, including the shepherd boy, Gruffydd, who told Grimbald what great stories there were to tell about him. He waved his crook in the air and shouted something in the Kournwahle tongue, which Grimbald took to mean farewell.

Inga kept running in and out of the house weeping. Wenslau and Bronwen were last to say goodbye to their household staff, some of whom were crying or trying hard not to, Eudda in particular. Bronwen, who was extremely sad, begged him to bring his sister back to the village. He told them it was quite possible she would come to the village eventually, but there was much to do and find out before he could bring her back. He knew that Agatha would have something to tell of great importance.

Wenslau grabbed hold of Grimbald by both arms and swore allegiance to him wherever he was and whenever he should need him. "Are you travelling entirely alone, my friend? Do you not want to take any of my men for your aid and company?"

"No, sire, many thanks, but I am at my best alone. I shall avoid all the other main towns and should be in Picheringa by nightfall. I intend to make further enquiries or see what

220

connects the town with Oolesby in Lindsey. I shall find Agatha; of that, I am most confident."

Some distance away in another shire, there was a battle raging between warring landowners around Rascill, half a day's ride from Eorforwic. Travelling along the main road was a heavily hooded priest with two young novices and two Huscarls from Coverham, heading for Eorforwic. The two warring parties were consequently suspicious of any strangers in the vicinity, and a small group of men from the west were scouring the forest and river. Unfortunately for the priest, he asked the Huscarls to stay guard while ordering his two novices to accompany him further into the woods. His intentions were notably vile to the soldiers, but they were getting well paid, and both decided to turn a blind eye to events. The hood came back to reveal the distinct coarse sandy brown hair of Barnard about to take advantage of the first young novice while the other was ordered to turn away. The priest was suddenly floored by a slingshot before he could put a hand on the young novice; he was knocked completely unconscious.

The two Huscarls heard a noise, thinking it was something related to Barnard, maybe a whip or something. Then there was a small scream. They both chuckled at one another. That was the last time they would be able to laugh for a while, for soon, they were surrounded by the men from Rascill. The two young novices were told to leave with a mule the group gave them, either to go back where they came from or seek refuge at Eorforwic. There were enough witnesses to Barnard's misdeeds that they decided a trial was unnecessary. He was taken to a yard, still unconscious, where livestock was kept, held over a trough, and castrated upon which his body writhed. He was then stripped bare and tied to a yoke fastened to two posts on the village green; his tonsure was tarred and feathered. He would have all sorts of vile things thrown at him, starve for three days, and be forced to beg for shelter and clothing. The two Huscarls were later tortured, and seeing the harsh justice meted out to Father Barnard, they did not delay in telling all. They, too, were stripped but given rags to wear; their horses, weapons, and money were taken from them for being associated with the evil priest. The leader of the clan told them to get away as fast as they could, as the other clan was even worse. The captors fell about laughing as the soldiers ran off into the distance as fast as they could. A young boy adept with the slingshot was asked to follow the raggy pair to ensure they did not try any tricks.

As the sun started to go down, Grimbald rode cautiously into Picheringa. Villagers going about their chores and friendly visits stared at him, most probably wondering if he was some kind of scout for an invading army. He nodded and tried to give a friendly air to his passage along the road. Soon he came upon an inn and managed to acquire a room and food for the night. The innkeeper told him to leave his horse with the stable boy after Grimbald took his saddlery and goods to his room. He wasn't the only traveller to far-reaching destinations. There were many traders heading for Eorforwic, some merchants just having a drink and food before camping with their market stalls and goods for the night.

The inn was soon alive with the smell and array of cooked meats and various types of bread, all freshly cooked, defying the least hungry to enjoy a morsel of something. Grimbald took his fill. Wenslau had given him a share of money from the battle with Wealdmaer and the purses of the evil murderers of his friends. That money he kept to one side, as there was a resonance to it, some information he could glean from its touch.

After his meal and a few beakers of ale, Grimbald asked the innkeeper, a big fat man with a mop of black hair who smelled of everything he touched. What did he know, and was there anyone with a connection to Lindsey that would regularly visit these parts?

"There are a good few, but where in Lindsey would you mean?"

"I believe it is a place called Oolesby," said Grimbald.

"Ah... well, there are two families that come from there. Both are traders. One, has a strange girl who never speaks... bonnie thing with pale yellow hair. I think she could be possessed, looks like a demon's inside there. But they don't always bring her along."

Grimbald's heart leapt an extra beat, "When do you expect they would next be here, sir?"

"I would say in the morning, early. Always here on Mondandaeg. Come here aftermarket for drinks and viddles."

Grimbald had a good few more ales before retiring, hoping to sleep, but too many thoughts were whirring through his mind. He was a tad wary of the innkeeper, who kept looking over him. He gave the innkeeper a story to stop him from prying or causing trouble, claiming he was on a special errand for King Aldfrith and utmost diligence had to be kept for his welfare. He said it in such a way that the innkeeper had no doubt it was true.

The next morning was beautiful, the sun beaming through the shutter as the cock crowed and the geese gaggled back and forth beneath Grimbald's window with the homeliest of farmyard smells. He was a little tired but had slept deeply. For morning fest, he would have two boiled goose eggs, with some rye bread to fill him for his journey and some of his own nettle tisane.

Having paid the innkeeper and tipped the stableboy for being honest, the knight set off for Oolesby after giving Aylmer a good fuss and a pat on the neck as he mounted. "Let's be off m' lad," he ordered as he nipped his heels into Almer's sides. As they trotted along the road., Grimbald suddenly thought if events hadn't turned out the way they did, he could have been a slave stable boy like the lad at Picheringa or worse. Or perhaps just tied to his uncle's farm with little hope of making anything worthwhile of himself. He immediately felt very lucky and proud of what he had been able to do.

Just a few miles down the road came a train of carts and wagons, horses, mules, donkeys, livestock, and trolleys full of vegetables and fruits. As was usual, local Huscarls led the way being tipped by the traders from their profits. Grimbald felt a sense of nostalgia for the journey his family had made all those years ago.

As the traffic was passing, he slowed as much as possible without stopping. He could not sense Agatha's presence but an overwhelming connection with a wagon only twenty-five yards further along. He rode up alongside to speak to the owner and could feel Agatha's aura on the front seat of the wagon. Grimbald explained who he was and knew his sister was with the family. In order to prove who he was and what gave him such knowledge, he demonstrated his skills with an object of theirs, to whom it belonged, and what had been done the day before. They were soon convinced and told him that she sometimes wouldn't move. The father had bought her at a slave market in Eorforwic two years ago, but she never spoke, so they nicknamed her Tadige (Toad). He further went on to say that she was at home with their daughter and a slave boy doing chores. "I've never whipped her!" said the man fearfully and then said, "I did pay good money for her. I hope you will have the grace to bear with me my loss if you are to take her?" Grimbald looked at him disapprovingly and said, "Then I hope this will be fair recompense." Knowing full well how much the man had paid. He accepted, with mouth wide open in astonishment.

Grimbald asked the man where their home was, "I just need to know roughly where?" he said.

In a little outhouse, a boy was hammering new wooden panels onto the rear of the building where the billy goat had been practicing his ramming techniques. This time the boy put some longer nails sticking out the other side as a deterrent. Suddenly a shadow loomed over his place of work, and a pretty young girl stood with a draft of ale in her hand, hovering near the boy's face. She gave half a smile, looking quite sad, then, without a murmur or movement, tears started to trickle down her cheeks.

"Tadige, what is wrong?" asked the boy as she froze on the spot, not even able to let go of the beaker.

"I- I – I do-o-o-n," she stammered.

"What is happening here? This pottery has to be ready for when mother and father get back, or there will be trouble…"

"Sh-sh… Kendra, Tadige was trying to spea," begged the boy.

"You do not shush me, scraggy, little slave boy. Get on with your work, and you come with me, Tadige. The woodshed needs cleaning out. Give him his drink, wipe your face, and get on with your chores.

Kendra was bossier than her mother and quite off-putting for most prospective husbands in the vicinity. She was mean but not nasty. Liking to look tougher than she was.

The house and small farm around it stood at the eastern end of the village near Clee and Thoresby villages. It seemed to be a haven for craftsmen and artists who mostly had their own croft or farm for sustenance.

It was mid-afternoon on that fine sunny day when a handsome warrior turned up at Kendra's gate. She had just caught sight of him through the window as he pulled up and quickly licked her fingers to straighten her stray locks before brushing herself down quickly to greet the stranger. She had just stepped off the doorstep when she saw him staring to her right, and Tadige stood staring back at him, sobbing with her arms outstretched.

Grimbald gave Aylmer's reins to Kendra, and she looked on in disbelief to see him grab Tadige in his arms. She spoke properly for the first time in years between sobs, saying quietly, "'Tis you, brother." Then overcome with emotion, she fell limply to the floor unconscious.

"Dearest Agatha, what has happened to you?" gasped Grimbald.

"So that's what she's called; I prefer Tadige," said Kendra haughtily.

"You do yourself no favours to afford such a jealous and unkindly manner," he observed.

"Jealous, I, nay sir, she is just dumb and simple," she added.

"You must have read my mind, young lass, for those are the words I had thought to describe you. You know nothing of the world, who I am, nor what my poor sister has been through, and I'd guess you know nothing about that poor young slave boy, save that you can kick him anytime you see fit. You have a goodness in you that I can see. Explore it, and you will be more attractive to those who have ignored you. I know your father is somewhat mercenary, but he did save my sister out of pity, even if he'd have you think otherwise."

Kendra was stunned, showed a white face, went inside, and started crying. The boy heard all the commotion and ran to see what he could do. Grimbald told him to see

Kendra, and he would watch over his sister. Agatha was looking more peaceful, though still unconscious; some of her past experiences were now coming to the fore. He could see the giant man fighting off some of the men who first kidnapped her, then how they felled him and left him for dead. Grimbald could see his face up close but could not be sure if he were dead or not; many of the images became cloudy as Agatha began to come around.

Inside the house, Kendra was still blubbing at being shamed and exposed in such a way when the young boy came in to ask if he could help. "Oh, bury your head in pig shit, Winfred" she screamed. Winfred did his best not to laugh as he could see this was another of her tantrums, but he was well pleased by who was the cause. Kendra thought about what the knight had said and slowly turned to look at Winfred, saying, "I am sorry, Winfred... go and enjoy your ale."

The boy was now stunned and nearly fell off the step he was half standing on.

As Agatha's eyes opened, her brother raised her forward to give her water and one of his herbal remedies to drink.

A few concerned neighbours had heard some commotion and came to see if there was any real trouble, giving the warrior a good-looking over. One old woman without a tooth in her head spluttered how they all looked out for each other and said what a great friend she was to most of the important people in these parts, especially the Abbot of Thoresby. So, he had better watch himself.

Grimbald smiled; how many times had he heard this kind of talk? "Would there be much in the way of work other than farming in this area, as you probably will know?"

The woman looked at him cautiously in case he was amusing himself at her expense and answered, "You could try Gyrwumsby. They need fishermen if you have done any or have an inkling, or there are the salt beds; always folk needed there. There's work for her, too, peat digging and washing; people always want washing. Aye, plenty of jobs. You'll need to rent a house, though, unless you can buy one," she sniggered.

Agatha started to feel better and had been amused by her brother's treatment of the old woman and, a little later, of Kendra. She began to remember him with his subtle sense of mischief, but with it came the anguish and pain that had brought them to this point. Agatha did not want to talk very much and allowed Grimbald to plan their journey with what few possessions she had and move on. They both decided she would ride on Aylmer with Grimbald until they reached the next town or village.

Winfred asked if he could help and if he would ever see Tadige again.

Agatha smiled sweetly at Winfred as they rode away and said in a soft voice, "Maybe?"

Kendra just looked on and waved goodbye, feeling slightly different, unlike the one that waved farewell to her father, mother, and family the previous evening.

CHAPTER TWENTY-FIVE

A Friend in Need

A person could smell Gyrwumsby for miles before seeing where it lay. There were all kinds of activities going on along the eastern road; trades and practices that were not common to Grimbald and his sister. There appeared to be a lot of opportunists and vagabonds, he would have to be on his guard, but there was something drawing him to this area. Agatha was very tired and needed a room and a comfortable bed for the night. The two had spoken quite a lot but mainly Grimbald. They would head for an inn close to the centre.

On the main thoroughfare, a blind man sat by the fence of a new church and said, "Look for the old Roman bathhouse; there is an old woman who'll take yer in. She needs the company and the money… if you can spare it. Me thinks you can."

Grimbald knew the old man told the truth and gave him three penningas. "Many thanks, sir."

"Sir, eh, don't often get that. Bless yer lad," replied the blind man.

The house was a mile further on; it was a large cosy, looking thatched roundhouse with a host of different animals in cages and traps. There were badgers, weasels, ferrets, a vixen with cubs, snakes, field mice, and toads, including three small dogs and a cat who roamed freely. Consequently, the whole place was a little smelly.

The thin, strong-looking old woman came to the doorway as Grimbald and Agatha arrived. He whispered to Agatha, "A Wiccan woman."

"I know, I was with one for months, but she drove me to despair with her hatred for other folk, always casting spells. I do not think she had much magic in her, just a bad spirit?" Agatha responded with slight trepidation.

"Brother and sister, eh, you can share the upstairs room at the front of the house for now. Are ye hungry both?"

The two were somewhat impressed at the lady's assumption about them.

"Are you feeling hungry, sister?" asked Grimbald.

"A little, but I feel more in need of a bed, I fear," sighed Agatha.

"Then you go to your bed, and I will bring a small meal up to you. Would you like a little something to make you feel at peace? I can make you a special draft."

The old woman overheard Grimbald and said, "I thought as much. I knew you were no ordinary soldier or king's man. We'll have to talk! Would the girl like a little baked fish with butter and vinegar? I've just made some fresh bread also, my own recipe. Perhaps you would like some meat?"

"Nay, Madam, I'll have the same as my sister. I thank you greatly."

The old woman knew he was eating lightly to have his wits about him, and he only wanted a jug of ale. "Will you sit with me at the table when you have seen to your sister? I get very few people here these days, and no one stays for long," she asked.

"Aye, Madam, I will," responded Grimbald sympathetically. He took the food and one of his tonics to Agatha, who was fast asleep by the time he arrived. There was a shelf on the wall with a small figurine which he thought strange; it gave him a sense of Mochanna being nearby. As it was at such a convenient height, he decided to leave Agatha's meal there. When he turned to go down the steps, Agatha awoke to say, "Many, many thanks, brother. I am so glad you found me. You have made me feel anew. I love you and want us to make something of our lives while we still have a chance. I think I need your help to feel truly alive again?"

"That, I promise, is my main goal, dear sister. I am here for you and only you at this moment. My master would probably disapprove, but I must make good with the only person I have left in our family."

"But have you forgotten Ulrich, and especially Edwin? He will probably be settled with his cousins and maybe even married now. I wonder if he will have heard about father and mother and what happened that horrible day. Do you know if Sunni and the other girl, I forget her name… did they survive?"

"Why yes, and Fyonn, they survived. I believe they are both with uncle Wynnstan. Sunni is back in Deira with my friend Wenslau. She was the one who told me about your location."

"That has made me feel so much happier, Grim. I cannot sleep now and want to tell you something important. I will eat this lovely-smelling fish and bread first." Grimbald sat on the bed beside her, watching her eat; they both kept smiling at each other as she ate heartily. He sensed her alertness was just a passing phase as she started to yawn and stretch before finishing her supper. "I shall tell all in the morning," she murmured as she let go of her plate and started to doze off. He pulled the cover over her and went down to join the old woman.

His place was set with bread, freshly cooked fish, and a nice draft of acorn wine, something he had not drunk for years, and it happened to be one of his favourite drinks.

The old woman sat opposite him with a beaker of the same wine; her dogs all sat beneath her. "Here's to fine weather, fine wine, and fine company," she said, raising her beaker in the air. Grimbald did likewise. And started to eat the delicious warm bread while she enquired how he came to choose her house to stay.

"Oh, twas the blind man by the church... he recommended you."

"I'm afraid you are mistaken young man, the only blind man hereabouts, died three years ago, trampled by stray cattle. Some folk say his spirit will not rest until he is offered a reward. He would always offer help to passing strangers, but nobody really showed him much respect."

Grimbald nearly choked on his bread. *Why did I not sense that? I have seen many spirits before,* he thought. Then a warm glow came over him as if some summer heat had wafted its way through the room. He realised this was a thank you for his unthinking generosity, and as he turned to look towards the door, three penningas were shining in the late day glow, laid neatly on the floor of the entrance.

The old woman looked at the focus of his attention and remarked, "Well, you do have a great spirit. I'll wager this will bring you and your sister much good fortune you'll need in times to come."

For the next two and a half years, Agatha and Grimbald made their home in Gyrwumsby. He went back to part-time fishing, and with the money he had from Wenslau, he set up a lodging house for foreign travellers which Agatha ran. Owing to his ways with herbs and medicine, Grimbald gained an ever-widening reputation. One thing he had not intended, though, was teaching the young gentry to fight.

He had inadvertently made a name for himself through a few awkward situations and very astutely putting them to rights.

The fishing was going exceedingly well, and sometimes there would be visits from his old friends from Jutland. They liked to say they were going to Great Grimbaldsby, and soon the name caught on. Many overseas traders started to do business in the town, but one type of trader Grimbald drove away with the help of the townsfolk, was slave traders. He spent quite a lot of his own money, and with the help of many locals, he managed to free the slaves. He told the slave traders that they should never show themselves anywhere near the town again, for which he had to do battle with the captain and some of his crew, single-handedly wounding them all but allowing them to leave. Everyone, bar one man in the town, backed him up and put fear into the trading party. Our hero had set the stall out that slavery was not to be encouraged, but it was not a popular proposal or venture for those of wealth and power.

There was one man in Grimbaldsby that resented 'this interloper' as he would call him. It would seem there was more than a hint of jealousy in him. Swidhun had been fishing from the port for most of his life before the stranger arrived and thought he deserved more recognition. He knew all the best places to fish and how to run a good business. Having ownership of many salt fields, he felt this newcomer could get in his way. In his view, Grimbald had to use the magic arts to do what normal folk spent years trying to master. The man had to be stopped.

On one balmy summer's morning, a trading ship set to port. Grimbald generally liked to know who was coming and going if he was not away fishing which did become less and less as his wealth increased. The fourth passenger to disembark was a tall man with a particular elegance about him. As he pulled back his hood, revealing a thick head of salt and pepper hair, he looked straight in Grimbald's direction. Here were two men so eager to embrace the friendship made all those years ago that could never be forgotten.

"GRIS," shouted Grimbald, "What a glory in my heart it is to see you."

"And I, you, Grimbald, I almost didn't recognise you. You look well apart from a few battle scars, lack of sleep, and overindulgence," joked Gris, slapping his friend on the shoulder, then hugging him. "You've actually turned out to be quite a handsome fellow, haven't you," he laughed.

"So, tell me... what is it that brings you to our town, you grey old buzzard?" as Grimbald asked the question, he could see Myrte in his mind's eye. She was in a worried state and seemingly in the middle of a battle.

"Well, apart from loving the smell of fish and the slime about my feet, tis you I wanted to see. You're reputation has sprung wide and far, my friend but then Myrte knew, as you would expect. Though more than this, she said your destiny is far from fulfilled. She needs your help in a war that has far-reaching consequences. We are to set sail as soon as you are able, and time is of the essence. I know you are curious to know more, but Myrte insisted we set sail before I inform you further. You will come, my friend?"

Grimbald was quite nervous about so much unknown to him at this time, but he sensed another connection to Mochanna once more. "Why yes, be sure of it, but I must make arrangements. You know what happened to our family?" Gris nodded sadly. "Wait until you see Agatha, I found her not far from here a few years ago, and together we have made a home for ourselves. She will not have a husband, though, but what can I say, I am not yet ready for a wife either. What have you done with yourself, Gris?"

"Ah well, there you have it. I have a wife, a mistress, and five children at the last count. So, I deserve some respite, don't you think? Can we get some decent ale or wine around here? I am in dire need of relaxation and a blurry head."

As the pair made their way through the busy streets, many people would greet Grimbald with admiration and respect, but he remained humble and always asked after their prospective families. Grimbald was just about to open the door to Agatha's lodging house when it flew open in his face, and a huge man came out with his head ducked in the doorway. "You people's go. No come back. No money, no work, no chance!" Out followed a couple of scruffy young men who had tried to pretend they had worked on one of the fishing boats and would settle their debt when they landed their next catch.

"Don't be too hard on them, Hrodhulf," asked Agatha softly as she followed behind, suddenly catching sight of

Grimbald and Gris. At this point, her tears started to well up in the corners of her eyes. "Oh, bless you, brother. When did you invite him? Oh, I am so sorry, Gris. Please do come in. It is so good to see you again."

"I did not invite him, sister. I am afraid my quiet days are suspended for now, as I am needed for a very important errand, and our friend has come to assist in our mission."

"I am afraid tis so young, Agatha. We must depart as soon as possible. By the gods, Grimbald, you did not tell what a beauty she has become. She must be Freya in human form," remarked Gris.

Gris had chartered a private ship to sail at first tide in the morning before returning to the lodging house where Grimbald and Agatha kept the best wines, cider, and ales. It wasn't long before Gris succumbed to Grimbald's favourite acorn wine, never having drunk it before. He would have a rather heavy head by the morning.

Early next morning, Grimbald and Gris said their farewells; Agatha pleaded with Gris to visit with family whenever they could. She gave both of them a big hug and reassured Grimbald that plenty of people could offer her support in his absence.

Once aboard the ship, Grimbald's first question was why such a large vessel for the two of them, suddenly realising that there would not be just two of them. Gris whispered to Grimbald, "There are only you, the captain, and myself, who know of our destination. We are stopping at Herewic to pick up some more men. Most of them are like yourself, trained in many disciplines and herbal lore; the rest are of exceptional fighting skills. We shall then change ships to sail on to the holiest of islands left in these waters, the Isles of Sylis, the last secret stronghold of the Druidda. There is much to do, my friend, and many dangers ahead of us, but with the gods on our side, we can bring lasting peace to the greater part of this world.

Clouds billowed, and the wind was in their favour as they sailed ahead into the German sea, but someone had been watching them and following from a distance.